GROWIN' UP IN '45

To Mark Cozad
—Max A. Geyer
12-14-08

GROWIN' UP IN '45

Max A. Geyer

Writers Club Press
San Jose · New York · Lincoln · Shanghai

ISBN: 0-595-00079-7

Published by Writers Club Press, an imprint of iUniverse.com, Inc.

For information address:
iUniverse.com, Inc.
620 North 48th Street
Suite 201
Lincoln, NE 68504-3467
www.iuniverse.com

URL: http://www.writersclub.com

CONTENTS

FOREWORD

The story *Growin' up in '45* is a semi-autobiographical sketch of the author's childhood adventures that he and a group of his teenage friends shared during the final year of World War II. The book provides exciting and very humorous reading, capturing the nostalgic allure of this bygone era.

The story takes place in 1945 in a small town in Indiana. The primary characters are a small group of adventuresome teenage boys, ranging in age from 13 to 15 years. Being naturally resourceful, this youthful band is able to fully utilize this period in time (from spring through winter of 1945) in finding excitement where they can and generally complicating their lives in the process. Their carefree attitudes lead them into moments of high adventure, total terror, as well as many hilarious situations.

The key characters are Reggie and Mark Gearing. Mark, the younger brother, is cast in the role of the storyteller. Reggie, the oldest and seemingly wisest member of this rowdy band of teenagers, is generally considered the group's leader. Reggie is kept busy planning future activities and settling disputes between the various members.

Other members of the gang are Spike, Wally, Pete, and Dan. Spike — most certainly the most mischievous of the group — is notable for his hair-trigger temper and ability to instigate trouble. Wally is the whimpish one; the one who is picked on much of the time, but who eventually is able to improve his image. Pete Rocelli, the policeman's son, stands out for his sarcastic nature and role as the resident prankster. Dan, who is destined to become a priest, also shares in some of the misadventures.

Without a doubt, the life-changing experiences that they encountered during 1945 significantly accelerated the "growin' up" process for these young men.

PREFACE

It was the spring of 1945, and World War II was winding down. Our country was about to receive an unconditional surrender from Germany, after which time we could concentrate our full war effort toward defeating Japan.

I personally didn't have any members of my immediate family serving in the armed forces, but I knew a lot of families who were well represented by sons, daughters, or fathers serving in one of the military branches.

My father, Kenny Gearing, at 41 was a little too old to be drafted. Furthermore, he was exempted from service because of the size of his family. He was the breadwinner for his wife, three sons, and a baby daughter. I'm not so sure he wouldn't have been drafted, though, had the war dragged on for another year.

Reginald (Reggie) was the oldest son and would be 15 in November. I was the second son and was christened Mark; I had turned 13 in January. My younger brother, Luke, was 6 years old. My little sister, Briggete, was within a couple of weeks of celebrating her third birthday.

My Mom, Marie, at 38 was still a beautiful woman. She was the consummate mother and wife — hard working, loving, and the perfect manager for a household of six.

She was truly the mainstay of the Gearing family. Not only did she manage all activities in the home, she was always there to advise and counsel each family member with their plans and problems. She was a wizard at managing what little income the family had during the depression. Without her financial mastery, we wouldn't have been living in the big, old house on the hill.

Dad Gearing, who was a little over 6-feet tall and a strapping 230 pounds, worked hard every day on his rural milk route.

Driving a large truck around the countryside in all kinds of weather, while stopping to load 120-pound milk cans from the dairy farms and then delivering the milk to the dairy, was exhausting, back-breaking work. He did this seven days a week, without complaint. On Christmas and Thanksgiving, Reg and I would ride with him and provide help in order to speed up the process. If we worked fast enough as a team, we could be home by 1:00 in the afternoon, in time for a turkey dinner with all the trimmings.

It took Reg and I together to heft a 10-gallon milk can up to the floor of the truck trailer. Sometimes, just to show off, Dad would swing one up with each hand.

On a typical working day, Dad arose about 4:00 in the morning and arrived home between 4:30 and 5:00 PM in the evening. He was generally exhausted and, understandably, didn't feel much like getting involved in family matters. He pretty much demanded peace and quiet in the evenings, and after supper, usually fell asleep in his chair, listening to one of his favorite radio programs.

A Movie to Remember

It was unseasonably warm and sultry that Thursday afternoon in April of 1945. Tomorrow would be Good Friday, and the students of Saint Matthew's would be starting their Easter vacation. I always looked forward to the spring break, because it meant six to eight days free from school.

It was something of a tradition for the good Sisters of Saint Matthew's to take their students to one movie during the school year. Of course, the movie had to have the proper religious values and meet the rigid moral standards set forth by the Catholic censorship organization, the Legion of Decency.

This movie we were about to attend was considered to be perfectly suited for the developing minds of sixth-, seventh-, and eighth-grade students. The three nuns who escorted us on our four-block walk down Main Street to the Harrison Theater seemed especially excited that this year's movie was to be "Going My Way." Why not? The movie was about priests and nuns, and I'm sure they secretly considered the male lead, Bing Crosby, about the biggest 'hunk' ever to don the priestly garb.

I was perspiring when we entered the theater and was therefore looking forward to the air-conditioned environment.

My eighth grade class was the first class to be seated. Probably because we were the oldest kids, we were given the prime location, about midway on the main floor.

I sat between my two best buddies, Walter "Wally" Fredericks and Clarence "Spike" Humphrey.

"It felt pretty damn good when we first came in here, but it's beginnin' to get a little chilly now," Wally whispered to no one in particular, as he swung his feet up on the seat in front him.

"Hey, watch your big feet, you stupid idiot. You're pulling on my hair!" exclaimed Mary Weaver, considered by some to be the homeliest girl in the eighth grade. Visibly embarrassed, Wally immediately dropped his feet to the floor and slumped way down in his seat, as all heads turned to see what was going on.

Two rows back, Sister Mary Clara barked, "What's going on up there?"

"Just a little accident, Sister. It won't happen again, I promise," replied Wally sheepishly.

"It had better not," she warned, loud enough for everyone to hear. "Now settle down and be quiet."

Just then the movie screen lit up, and the newsreel was on.

"Hope we see some gals in bathing suits," commented Wally.

"Yeah, like Betty Grable," I replied.

"Best legs in the world," Spike chimed in.

I don't think any of us were prepared for what we were about see.

The newsreel started out with the latest film from the war in the pacific. The marines had just established a beachhead on one of the islands and were fighting their way into the jungle. Offshore ships were laying down a heavy barrage of artillery fire in front of the marines. The troops were moving slowly through the jungle, rifles at the ready. Once in awhile, a Japanese sniper was shown being shot out of the top of a palm tree. The boys my age really ate up this kind of war action, especially when it was apparent we had the enemy on the run.

The scene changed to a squad of marines who had just confronted heavy fire from a bunker in the side of hill. While their buddies provided cover fire to keep the enemy pinned downed, two marines approached the bunker with flame-throwers in an attempt to flush out the occupants. Both of the marines began spraying the cave with long bursts of flame. Although the boys in our crowd cheered wildly at the action unfolding, I'm sure the nuns didn't find the brutality very enjoyable.

And then it happened! As the smoke cleared, we were given our first glimpse of two of the cave dwellers. There seemed to be one loud gasp as we first viewed the naked Japanese man and woman who had exited the cave, with their hands raised high.

Apparently, there had not been much of an effort to airbrush out the frontal body parts. Nervous giggling ensued.

Spike blurted out, just loud enough for Wally and me to hear, "Holy shit! Naked Japs!"

Sister Mary Clara murmured prayerfully, "Jesus, Mary, and Joseph."

Expecting more Japanese to exit the cave in some form of undress, Sister Mary Margaret jumped from her seat down front, turned around and screamed, "Cover your eyes, children!" Of course the command came too late. We had already seen the good stuff. From then on, it was just a few fully clothed Japanese soldiers who came out to surrender to the marines.

Everyone was really quiet throughout the rest of the movie. I guess we all felt embarrassed for the nuns and were uncomfortable with the thought that we may have to confront the newsreel episode later at school.

The main feature, *Going My Way*, lived up to its billing. It was a great movie, but I think, for most of us, and especially the nuns, the newsreel kind of overshadowed the spiritual benefits of the movie.

To everyone's relief, nothing was ever mentioned at school about the newsreel incident.

It wasn't until much later that I learned it was not uncommon for the Japanese soldiers to have their so-called "Comfort Women" with them. It then dawned on me that the naked couple in the newsreel hadn't just been cleaning rifles together.

Communing with Nature

It was about 11:00 o'clock Good Friday morning, and my brother Reggie and I had finished our household chores for Mom, and the rest of the day was ours to spend as we pleased. (The weekly house cleaning was normally done on Saturdays, but this week, Mom wanted to get it done early in preparation for Easter.)

Some of the guys were waiting on the front porch for us to finish our work. Most of them had older sisters to do the weekly sweeping, mopping, dusting, and window cleaning chores. Reg and I thought they had it made, not to have to do *girls'* work.

As Reg and I stepped outside, Spike said sarcastically, "It's about time. Most of us have been out here for about an hour."

Pete Rocelli, another kid from the neighborhood and a policeman's son, added, with a smirk on his face, "Well, you know what they always say: *A woman's work is never done.*" The other two guys, Wally Fredericks and Dan McClure, laughed uproariously.

"Knock it off, you guys, or I'm gonna kick some asses," Reg said, feigning anger. "We can't help it that we don't have no older sisters. You can talk to my Mom and Dad about that."

I interrupted by saying, "We're wastin' time. What do you guys wanna do?"

"Let's head out to the College Woods," Dan suggested. Everyone agreed instantly.

The woods that backed up the Harrington College campus along its east side was nearly a quarter-mile deep in the easterly direction and approximately two miles in length, along a north-south line. A fairly large creek formed the eastern boundary of the College Woods. In turn, the creek was bounded on its east side by the Erie Railroad tracks.

The rock bed underneath the railroad tracks was mounded up about four feet, with a cinder pathway on either side. The railroad track was elevated well above the creek, in some places forming a steep, 60-foot embankment that ran down to the edge of the creek. The creek ran parallel with the tracks for almost the entire length of the woods.

Immediately to the east of the railroad tracks began the rural farming area that bordered the northern city limits of Harrington, Indiana. (Spike's father was an engineer for the Erie Railroad; Dan's worked as a conductor for the same company.)

We usually entered the woods from the south end, which was only about a quarter-mile east of the Gearing house.

The south edge of the College Woods was adjacent to the Harrington Laboratories, a small industrial complex. All of us resented the fact that the Lab emptied their chemical waste products into the southmost end of the creek, before it flowed into the Harrington sewer system.

Fortunately, **our** part of the creek was located to the north of the Lab's spill.

None of us was too surprised to find that the creek was swollen to the top of its banks as a result of the four days of heavy rain we'd had. We all stopped momentarily, and pondered the turbulent water as it roared downstream, sweeping with it large, fallen tree limbs that were caught up in the raging waters. None of us had ever seen the creek look so menacing.

The sky had begun to look threatening as we neared the entrance to the woods. Once inside the woods, we proceeded along the main pathway next to the creek, as even more black clouds formed above us.

"Geez, I hope it doesn't rain again today," said Dan. "It seems like that's all we've had this spring."

Dan McClure, who was from a good Irish-catholic family, was also an eighth-grader at St. Matthews and was making plans to enter a seminary in the fall. Although Dan was convinced he had received the "Calling", I had a difficult time actually visualizing him as a priest. Heck, he'd done all the same bad things I'd done, maybe some even worse.

As we progressed deeper into the woods, I observed that the spring wild flowers were in full bloom, and their sweet fragrance was very much in evidence. I secretly wished I could pick some for Mom, but I knew that would get me a ribbing from the other guys. " *Maybe I'll come back later and get her some,*" I thought to myself.

"Let's go back to the swamp area and see how bad it's flooded," said Reggie.

"Okay, but maybe it's too deep to move around in very easy," suggested Spike.

Wally broke through the thicket first, and yelled, "Would you look at this? Little islands all over the place."

As all six of us stood at the edge of the swamp and gazed in wonderment, Spike exclaimed, "We oughta be able to do somethin' real good with this setup! Whaddya think, Reg?"

"Well, we could each have our own little kingdom and then have battles to take over the other kingdoms," Reggie replied. "Okay, everybody, pick out an island."

Since the water at its deepest point was only four or five inches above shoe-top level, none of us got too wet in wading to our island of choice. It turned out that the six islands roughly formed a circle, and they ranged from about 8 to 12 feet apart.

As we stood looking at each other from our island "Kingdoms", Spike said, "This is stupid. What are we 'sposed to do now?"

Just then, Wally turned his back on everyone and began unzipping his trousers.

"Hey, Wally, whatcha doin'?" Reggie yelled.

"Takin' a leak. What the hell does it look like?" Wally responded in an irritated voice.

"Well, don't waste all of it. I have an idea." Reggie said excitedly. "I have a plan how we can make war with each other. The first guy who can piss the longest and enough to hit every other island with his "Rocket Launcher" will be the conqueror. He'll be declared the Supreme Ruler, and everybody else will have to do his bidding the rest of the day. How's that sound?" Everyone seemed to like the idea.

"Who goes first?" Pete asked impatiently. "We sure as hell can't draw straws from this far apart."

"How 'bout usin' first names in alphabetical order?" I suggested.

"I know, we'll use Mark's idea, only let's do it in reverse alphabetical order," Reggie countered. *Reg always has to be different,*" I thought to myself.

"Okay, but let's just get it started, " Pete said, eagerly. "It looks like Wally goes first."

"Hell, that ain't fair, fellas," Wally whined. "You stopped me right in the middle of my pee, and I'm probably already outta ammo."

Reluctantly, Wally readied himself, and launched his first burst toward Pete's island.

"Christ, that's pathetic, Wally. You only made it half way here." Pete chortled.

"Yeah, and now I'm finished. This game ain't no fun," Wally complained.

"Guess it's my turn," Spike said, as he launched a rocket into Reggie's island. "Wow, did ya see that," he crowed.

"Don't get all swelled up. You still got four to go," Reggie warned.

Spike was able to reach Dan's island and almost reach mine, before both pressure and quantity faltered.

Reggie, by now, was standing at the ready. "Okay, here goes," as he aimed at Dan's property.

Dan had to jump sideways to keep from getting hit.

"Helluva of shot, Reg", Pete said, admiringly.

With a grin, Reggie said, "You're next, Pete," as he launched a stream Pete's way, barely hitting the edge of Pete's island.

Reggie was able to hit both Wally's and my islands, but fell short of Spike's.

It was Pete's turn, and he looked confident. "You'd better run for cover, Reg," he yelled, as he let go with a good shot, making Reggie jump to the edge of his island to keep out of range of the deadly liquid.

Pete then directed his firepower toward Spike and actually hit one of his shoes.

"Boy, you're gonna pay for that one," threatened Spike.

Pete blasted my island and Dan's before he "petered" out.

I did better than I expected. I was able to reach Reggie's, Pete's, and Dan's islands before I ran out of juice.

The big surprise was Dan. He hit every island with extraordinary accuracy and pressure. If you didn't know better, you'd guess he had been saving up his supply of urine for days. It was awesome!

Dan's last target was Wally's empire. After pausing to take careful aim, he launched a long, yellow stream that seemed to arc 15 feet in the air. Wally ran from one side of his island to the other, attempting to evade Dan's laser-like barrage. Wally was finally teetering on the water's edge, when he caught the last bit of the geyser full in the face, driving him back until he began losing his balance. "Kersplash," he went, as he landed flat on his back in the muddy water. He came up quickly, sputtering and cussing, as we all convulsed in laughter.

"Dan, you're gonna make one helluva priest," Spike said.

"Yeah, you can hear my confession anytime," I added.

"What am I gonna do? I'm soakin' wet," Wally lamented.

"Aw, quit your whinin', Wally," Spike responded in an annoyed tone. "You'll dry off in a little while."

Pete turned to Dan and said, "Well, okay, your Majesty, what do you wish your subjects to do for you?"

Dan replied in a low growl, "I'm hungry. Bring me f-o-o-o-d!"

"Well, it's too early in the spring to raid gardens," Reg commented.

"How 'bout roast chicken?" asked Spike.

"How are we gonna pull that off?" I inquired.

"I've gotta plan," Spike replied. "Let's go up on Suicide Hill and plot our strategy."

Soon we were back on the main path, heading north, deeper into the woods. The sun was beginning to show itself, as the storm clouds moved farther east.

As we walked along the path, I began reflecting on my first experience with Suicide Hill.

It was the week after Christmas in 1940. I was almost 9, and Reg had recently turned 11. We each had received brand new, sleek, 5-foot long, American Flyer sleds as Christmas gifts, and were anxious to try them out on the "real" thing.

About 8 inches of new snow had accumulated over a three-day period, and temperatures during the day hovered around 15 degrees. Sledding conditions were perfect, especially where the snow had been packed down from usage, turning the top to ice.

We had been experimenting on some smaller slopes on the streets near our house and were satisfied that our new sleds were not to be equaled in the neighborhood. Our sled runners and steering mechanisms were broken in nicely. Not only could we "fly" down Finley Street hill, which ran southward along the side of our house, we could also "turn on a dime" at the bottom of the hill. We were ready for **Suicide Hill**!

Reg and I had been bugging Mom for a couple of years for permission to try out Suicide Hill. Unfortunately, she too, had heard the horror stories about the killer hill. This year, however, she begrudgingly relented, with a final warning, "If you get hurt, don't come home."

Needless to say, we were both pretty excited as we headed up Finley Street with our sleds in tow; and I must admit, we were more than just a little apprehensive at the prospect of our trip down the hill.

The top of old "Suicide" was roughly on the same level as our property on Finley Street, and about one-quarter of a mile to the north.

Reg and I had progressed past the last house on Finley Street, which was two blocks from our house, when we stepped into the thickly over-grown field that marked the southern boundary of the Harrington College wilderness area. Immediately to our right was the west edge of the College Woods.

As we walked along the path that ran next to the edge of the woods, my heart began to pound wildly. We were getting close to the **Hill**.

I could now see the path at the top of hill, looming about 200 feet in front of us. A figure had exited the path and turned our way.

As we got closer to the boy dragging his demolished sled, we could hear him sobbing softly. He was probably about Reg's age and was limping badly and holding a handkerchief to his bloody nose.

After we passed him, I looked up at Reg, and said, "Do ya still think this is a good idea?"

Reg didn't answer. I assumed he was deep in thought, trying to steel himself for what was about to come.

The scene from the top of Suicide was chaotic. Some kids were at the top beginning their slides or waiting their turn; some were scream-ing loudly as they flew down the hill; others were climbing back up the steep path along side the icy sled course; and still others had completed their slides and were picking up their sleds to go at it again. All in all, there must have been close to 50 adventurous youngsters participating in the "fun." Most of them looked to be of high-school age, and all appeared to be older than Reg.

We stood in back of the small group of kids who were awaiting their next slide. I observed that each kid, as his turn came up, would take a running start and then flop belly-down on their sleds, in order to gain maximum speed.

The slide part of the hill was very narrow, maybe 12-feet wide, with a small footpath formed on one side. The sled course was lined by trees on each side, which made it especially hazardous.

The slope itself was actually divided into two parts. The first steep grade ran downhill for about a 150 feet before meeting a slight step; then it dropped precipitously for another 200 to 250 feet before leveling off. The level part of the slide-way was a straight run of another 300 feet or so before it ran into the frozen College Park creek.

As we approached the front of the line, I turned to Reggie and asked, "Which way are you gonna do it, sittin' up or layin' down?"

Reg, apparently having been pondering the same question, replied, "Well, sittin' up, you can smash into somethin' face-first." "Layin' down, you could hit head-first and break your neck."

I gulped, and said, "If you don't mind, let's go down together the first time."

"Okay, we'll go double, sittin' up," Reggie replied. "But we're takin' your sled."

We had finally worked our way to the front of the queue. I took the front seat, with my feet positioned on the front metal portion of the sled. Reg sat behind me, with his legs straddling my hips. His legs were long enough for his feet to rest comfortably on the wooden cross-member used for steering. My life would be literally resting in his feet.

Reggie looked around at that kid directly behind us, and said, "Give us a shove, will ya?"

The kid said "Sure," and placed his hands on Reggie's shoulders and began pushing us as fast as he could toward the edge of the slope. Suddenly, we were off and running and accelerating rapidly.

Something that Reggie and I hadn't counted on, though, was the fact that the weight of two passengers made the sled go even faster than we'd observed with the other kids' slides.

We had already gained considerable speed when we hit the natural step in the course. There was a violent bump as we momentarily leveled out and then we became airborne as we flew off the knee of the step. At that moment, as we glided six feet above the steep incline, I became aware that we were actually higher than the tops of the trees that lined the course below us.

We were probably in flight for 20 feet before we nosed down enough to make contact with the icy incline again. We hit hard on the right runner, and were swerving toward the trees, when Reggie yelled frantically, "Lean left, Mark!"

Responding to his command, I threw my weight to the left as hard as I could, while maintaining a white-knuckled grip on the handrail. Both sled runners finally made contact with the ground again, and, after some wild wobbling, Reggie was able to gain control of the sled. Once back on the track, we were moving straight and fast, almost as if we were somehow "jet-propelled." Feeling we were no longer in imminent peril, I was able to take my first breath since we had started our downhill adventure.

We were now at the bottom of the hill, but still going at a blinding speed. The trees on either side were a blur. It was obvious now that we wouldn't get stopped in time to avoid the creek, and we were going much too fast to jump off. Turning into the trees was totally out of the question. We'd just have to ride it out.

The edge of the creek came up fast, and we were once again airborne as we catapulted off the top of the 4-foot bank.

We hit the ice for only an instant, skipped, and with a tremendous impact, buried the front of the sled in the other bank, causing me to slide forward and crash face-first into the hard dirt. The forward thrust of Reggie's weight added to the force of my impact. Everything went black.

As the cobwebs cleared slowly from my head, I could hear Reggie yelling frantically, "Are you okay, Mark? Are you okay?"

I finally replied weakly, "Uh-huh." "At least, I think so."

"Damn! You scared the hell out of me," Reggie said nervously. "Ready to go again?"

"Are you crazy?" I asked incredulously.

I had learned two important lessons that day: don't go down old Suicide in the sitting-up position with two on a sled; but if you think you have to, **don't** be the guy in the front.

Except for the face full of dirt, and the few moments that I'd been rendered insensible, I came through it pretty well. Although, I did leave a pretty good impression of my face in the side of the bank.

After the brief flashback, I began thinking of the roast chicken idea that Spike had come up with. I wondered to myself, "Was he talking about some left-over chicken that we could cop from his refrigerator?"

Our "gang of six" finally reached the foot of Suicide Hill. It would be in the clearing at the top of the hill that we would plan our next move. This was the spot where we always gathered to "pow-wow" during our outings in the woods. The location also kept us close to an artesian spring, which was located on the same hill that formed Suicide, only about 100 feet farther north.

Access to the natural spring was provided by a path that intersected at the same point as the natural step in Suicide's formation, which was about one-third of the way down the hill.

Long ago, someone had buried a 12-inch diameter clay tile straight down into the spring's outlet, so that clear, cool water was always available at the brim of the tile. A water supply was an important factor if you were to survive all day in the woods.

As we stood in clearing at the top of Suicide, I asked, "Okay, Spike, we go to your house and steal the left-over chicken, right?"

"Hell no, we steal a chicken from a chicken pen on the other side of the railroad tracks," Spike, visibly annoyed, replied sharply.

"Okay, say we get us a live chicken, how do we get it ready for eatin'?" inquired Reggie.

"Well, I guess I'll just hafta lay it all out for you guys," Spike said, showing his irritation. "We got spring water, and I'm sure we can find an old bucket at the dump site down by the creek. And to top it off, I got plenty of dry matches for makin' a fire to heat up the water. So that's all we need to get the feathers off."

"Okay," Wally said, looking puzzled. "So now we got ourselves a naked chicken."

"Dammit, I'm not through yet," Spike barked. "Any fool knows you gotta butcher 'em. Pete's got his huntin' knife, and Reg and Mark have helped their Mom clean chickens before. We got all we need, except for the chicken, right?"

We all nodded in agreement.

"But who steals the chicken?" Dan asked.

"I guess me and Mark can handle that," Spike said. "The rest of you guys can get busy finding us a good bucket and some fire wood, and be sure to have a spit ready when we get back."

"What's a spit?" Wally asked.

Spike seemed infuriated with the last question, and showing his exasperation said, "Christ, guys, tell him, will ya?" "I don't have time for anymore of this bull shit. Let's go, Mark."

Spike and I left the other guys and proceeded down the hill. I checked my watch and noted it would be one o'clock in 15 minutes. We had plenty of time. As far as I knew, none of us had to be home before 5 o'clock, in time for the evening meal.

Our spirits sagged as we stood staring at the creek. Spike and I had forgotten just how deep and turbulent the water was.

"Well, I guess that about does it," mused Spike. "There's no way we can cross here, and if we go clear back to the Harrington Labs and cross over at the highway, it'll cost us a half-an-hour."

"Wait a minute," I interrupted. "What about going upstream a little ways, where the old fallen tree is?"

"It's worth a try," Spike responded.

A large tree had fallen across the creek several years before, and had formed a natural bridge across the 30-foot span of water. The tree had once stood about 20 feet from the bank on our side of the creek, and the big roots that had been ripped from the ground towered 15 feet in the air.

The tree's trunk was about 4-foot wide. About half way across the span, the first limbs protruded, forming natural handholds. Of course, the most treacherous part was getting from our bank to where the tree limbs began.

We stood for a moment surveying our "bridge" and the foaming water that surged beneath it.

I noticed that the bark of the tree was still saturated with water. A slippery footing would even make matters worse.

Before Spike could say anything, I said a little nervously, "Let me go first." For some reason, I dreaded the thought of being the last one to go across.

I used some of the roots to hoist myself up on the trunk. I was then able to stand up and begin inching my way to the other side.

My heart was pounding wildly as I took my first few steps over the water. I thought to myself, *"Once I reach the limbs, I'll be okay."*

About half way to the limbs, my right foot slipped off the walkway, causing my upper body to begin swaying over the raging water. Using my outstretched arms as a counterbalance, I was able, after a few anxious moments, to stop the swaying and regain my footing.

Three more quick steps, and I was able to grab a limb and pull myself forward to a more secure position.

"Okay, Spike, your turn." I yelled. "I'll stay here and grab your hand when you get close enough."

For some reason, Spike was very quiet as he boarded the tree trunk.

He actually was doing better than I had done, until he had progressed to about four feet from the limbs, where I stood waiting with my right arm extended toward him.

Suddenly, Spike began to lose his balance. At the moment he began slipping off the right side of the tree, he made a desperate leap toward me. Our right hands connected, and my firm one-hand grip caused Spike to swing toward me with his legs dangling knee-deep in the turbulent water. The force of the current began pulling his lower body away, stretching my grip to the breaking point. Spike, although a few inches shorter than me, weighed approximately the same — about 120 pounds.

I knew I couldn't hold him with one hand much longer.

"Please, Lord, give me the strength to do this," I said to myself.

As our hands began slipping apart, Spike looked up at me wild-eyed, and said pleadingly, "Don't leave go, Mark."

I kept as firm a grip as I could, as I hooked my left leg around the upright limb that I had been hanging onto. In this position, I was able to bend forward enough to reach his left hand with mine. As our left hands touched, I lunged a little farther forward and got a good grip. Our arms were momentarily crisscrossed. Then, with a twisting motion, our arms straightened out, leaving Spike waist-deep in the water, with his back toward me.

I leaned my left shoulder heavily into the limb as I pulled upward with all my strength. Spike was coming out of the water. I finally had him to a point where his butt rested on top of the trunk. As I freed his left hand, he grabbed the limb I'd been holding onto, and together we pulled him all the way onto the walkway.

From there, it took us only an instant to clear the other branches of the tree bridge and jump down to the solid ground.

Once on the ground again, Spike grabbed me in a bear hug and said, "Thanks, Buddy."

I noticed his eyes were a little watery as I replied, "That's okay, Spike."

We both knew how lucky we'd been.

Straight ahead was the railroad embankment. On the other side were the small farms that backed up to the railroad property.

As we stood on the railroad ties at the top of the embankment, Spike pointed down and said, "See, what did I tell ya." "There's a chicken coop right down there."

Sure enough, directly in front of us was a chicken house with a fenced-in area filled with chickens.

We sneaked down the embankment as quietly as we could, and crept along side the fence until we had reached the gate. Right outside the gate, strewn on the ground, were kernels of corn that must have been dropped during an earlier feeding.

As he picked up a handful of corn, Spike whispered, "This is what we're gonna use to coax the chickens to us. When a chicken comes close enough, you grab him by the neck."

As we crouched along side the fence, Spike thrust his hand palm-up through the a square opening near the bottom of the chicken wire. "Here, chickee, chickee. Here, chickee, chickee", he repeated softly.

Finally, an old Bard Rock hen became curious enough to investigate. She was just about to pick a piece of corn from Spike's hand, when I grabbed her neck.

From there on, I had to elevate her hand-over-hand through the square-mesh openings in the fence. Each time I released my grip to grab the neck with the other hand, the chicken would squawk loudly, until my grip could be tightened again.

I thought to myself, *"With all this noise, someone is bound to hear us."*

Sure enough, an old lady came out the back door of the farmhouse screaming, "What's going on out there!"

We had been caught red-handed!

Just as the old lady seemed about to close the distance between us and the house, I was able to clear the top of the fence with the chicken.

"Let's go!" I yelled at Spike, and we began running up the embankment, toward the safety of the woods.

The chicken was still squawking as we reached the railroad track at the top of the embankment.

Down the other side we ran, stumbling and sliding as we went.

I could now hear male voices joining with the old lady's.

We were so scared and running so fast that later I could not even remember crossing the "tree bridge."

Not willing to risk the perilous crossing, the "posse" gave up the chase at the creek's edge.

Spike and I continued running toward Suicide Hill, as I maintained a death grip on the old chicken's neck.

When the other guys saw us running up Suicide, Pete yelled, "Do you believe it? They got a chicken!"

Spike and I were out of breath when we joined the guys at the top of the hill.

For the first time, I became aware that the old chicken hadn't squawked for a while. In fact, she hadn't even moved for a while. The full realization hit me that she'd died somewhere along the way, probably due to my carrying her by the neck. I felt a twinge of guilt and sadness as I handed her lifeless body over to Reg.

All of sudden, roast chicken didn't sound so good anymore.

Reggie held the chicken up by the feet and said happily, "How about this, fellas? We won't even have to kill it."

The guys had the fire going good, and the 5-gallon bucket of water that sat on the rocks encircling the fire was beginning to steam. It wouldn't be long until the water came to a boil.

A second bucket of fresh water sat off to the side of the fire. This would be used for dressing (butchering) the de-feathered chicken.

Two forked sticks of the same height had been pushed securely into the ground on opposite sides of the fire bed. The forks would provide the cradle for the spit, upon which the chicken would ultimately be skewered.

I took note of the spit that was laying nearby on the ground. It had been fashioned from a small-diameter, 3-foot tree branch. One end had been sharpened, and the branch ran arrow-straight for about two feet before it connected with what was left of a crooked branch, approximately one foot in length. The crooked portion would provide a natural hand crank for turning the spit.

The water was now boiling furiously.

"Hey, Wally, hand me that tree branch layin' next to you," Reggie said. "We can use that to get the bucket off the fire. Here, grab the other end as I pass it through the handle."

Reggie and Wally, each holding opposite ends of the limb, lifted up the bucket of scalding-hot water and carried it to a level, clear spot, about ten feet from the fire.

"Okay, fellas, gather 'round, this is the good part," Reggie said, as he held the old chicken by the feet and plunged it deep into the steaming water.

He repeated the dunking process several times, before saying, "Okay, everybody grab a handful of feathers."

As Wally got up close to the chicken, he exclaimed, "Whoo-wee! What the hell is that rotten smell?"

"For Chris' sakes, Wally, ain't you never smelled a wet chicken before?" Pete replied, in an agitated voice.

With everyone pitching in and grabbing a handful of feathers after each hot-water dunk, the old chicken was completely de-feathered in about five minutes.

As Reggie laid the chicken on one of the flatter rocks that surrounded the fire pit, he yelled, "Hey, Pete, throw me your huntin' knife. We're gonna gut this old gal now."

Always the wise guy, Pete responded by throwing the knife from about ten feet away. The knife stuck in the ground about four inches from Reggie's left foot.

Reggie jumped to his feet, and said angrily, "You dumb shit!" "You coulda chopped some of my toes off. If I had the time, I'd kick your ass right here."

"Sorry, Reg," Pete replied quickly. "You know I wasn't tryin' to stick ya."

"Well, Okay," Reggie responded. "But if you ever try that again, I'll shove that knife so far up your ass, they'll hafta blast it out with dynamite."

Reggie picked up the knife and chopped off the chicken's feet. He then began sawing its head off. A couple of the guys groaned. Wally was beginning to turn white.

"You want the chicken head?" Reggie asked tauntingly, as he threw it at Wally.

Wally jumped as if someone had shot at him, in order to avoid the "deadly" chicken head.

Man, don't do that shit." "I don't feel too good, anyway," Wally whined mournfully.

The rest of us laughed gleefully.

Next, Reggie made a broad slit under the chicken's tail. He then placed the knife down, and thrust his hand deep into the rear opening he had made. When he withdrew his hand, it was apparent he had just disemboweled the old chicken. In his hand was an unsightly glob of blood and guts, which he threw on ground beside him. (I could tell Reggie was really enjoying this. His audience was spellbound.)

Most of the guys groaned in unison. "E-e-e-Yuk!" responded Wally, who was noticeably pasty-faced and unsteady on his feet.

Reggie then made a vertical slit above the chicken's breastbone and removed the craw (stomach) and what lungs were left. These entrails joined the others on the ground.

It was apparent that the appetites were going fast.

As the final step in the cleaning process, Reggie dunked the old chicken several time in the fresh-water bucket, and, while the chicken was immersed in the water, he rubbed his hand vigorously around the inside and outside to remove any remaining undesirable parts.

With the old chicken pretty well cleaned and hollowed out, Reggie skewered the carcass from front to back with the spit and rested the two ends of the spit in the forks of upright sticks.

All we had to do now was keep turning the spit slowly until the bird was done to a 'golden brown'.

I looked at my watch; it was almost 3:15. We had been roasting the chicken for almost an hour.

The breast of chicken, which protruded farthest into the fire on each rotation, was beginning to turn black.

While poking the chicken with a short stick, Spike said excitedly, "I think this baby's about ready to eat. Whadda you guys think?"

It was apparent that everyone was hungry again and beginning to get a little impatient.

"Well, I think the breast part is the most done," Reggie replied. "We'll let Dan have the first bite. It's his party."

Reggie held the spit steady with his left hand, as he used Pete's knife to slice away a piece of the breast meat. He handed the piece of meat to Dan, saying, "Try this, your Majesty."

Our mouths were watering as we watched Dan take his first bite.

"U-m—m-m, this is real tasty," Dan proclaimed. "My compliments to the Chef. You can give some to the other fellas now, Reg."

Reggie continued cutting away the breast portion and serving the individual slices until everyone had a piece to munch on. We all sat there eating, each of us savoring our tasty piece of white meat.

"Man, this was a great idea you had, Spike." Pete commented. " I never knew chicken could taste so good."

It was apparent Wally had gained back his appetite. He had 'wolfed' down his piece of chicken and was sitting there waiting for another piece. When his next portion was not forthcoming, he picked up the hunting knife and began to help himself to a drumstick. I guess he felt, at this point, it was every man for himself.

Wally took his first big bite of the drumstick. A look of contentment spread across his face, as he munched heartily on the first tasty mouthful. "Man, it don't get no better than this," he mused.

All of sudden, Spike jumped up, pointed at Wally, and exclaimed, "For Chris' sakes, there's blood runnin' out the side of your mouth! I think I'm gonna be sick."

Wally, threw his chicken leg in the fire, and began spitting violently to cleanse his mouth. As he spat out the masticated chicken pulp, he could see some of the large quantity of blood that had been in his mouth; he had swallowed the rest.

His face took on a greenish cast as he ran for the nearest bushes. We could hear the gagging sound, followed by a long "U-r-r-r-r-p" and then a prolonged splash, as Wally emptied the contents of his stomach on the ground.

Those of us who still had some chicken left threw it in the fire.

"Well, I'm full. How 'bout you guys?" Reggie asked.

Dan answered first, "Yeah, Reg, I'm stuffed. Couldn't eat another bite."

The rest of us all nodded our agreement. Who really felt like eating now?

We hadn't counted on the fact that the breast meat could be so well-done, while the rest of the bird remained virtually in a raw state.

We all agreed it was time to wind up the day's activities, and began cleaning up our fire site. The remains of old chicken, still on the spit, were thrown into the fire. The fire bed was then covered liberally with loose soil.

As we walked south through the brush field, toward the Finley Street, Spike asked, "Whadda we goin' to do for excitement tonight?"

Reggie replied, "Let's just go downtown and hang out...play some pool, or somethin." "Mark and me don't have much money, so a movie's out."

"We can watch the big guys cruisin' Main Street...maybe even meet some girls along the way," I added.

Pete, Dan, and Wally were bummed out because they didn't think they could get out on this particular Friday night.

We were now at the corner of Finley and Kimmel, where the Gearing house was located. This is where we would split up. Spike had the farthest to go home, maybe twelve blocks southeast. Pete, Dan, and Wally all lived within five blocks of our house.

As we split up to go our separate ways, Reggie yelled at Spike, "Me and Mark'ull meetcha down in front of the Harrison Theater at 7:00. Okay?"

"I'll be there," Spike replied, looking back over his shoulder.

As Reggie and I walked into our enclosed back porch, the wonderful smell of home-cooking met our nostrils. It was getting close to 5:00 o'clock, and Mom would have supper on the table pretty soon.

We stepped through the kitchen door, and Mom, busily working at the stove, greeted us with a smile, and said, "What have you boys been up to today?"

"Aw, nothin' much, Mom," Reggie replied, as he looked my way with a devilish grin on his face.

Mom was frying salmon patties in one skillet and fried potatoes in the other. The salad was ready and waiting.

I couldn't wait to start eating. Salmon patties was one of my favorite dishes, and I was famished. It was certain that the little bit of chicken I'd eaten earlier hadn't satisfied my hunger pangs.

"You boys get washed up now. Supper will be ready in about five minutes," Mom said.

Reggie and I went directly to the bathroom, which was right off the kitchen, and washed off some of the grime that had been collected during the day's outing.

As we walked by Mom again, she said, "Tell your Dad and the other kids that supper will be on the table in couple of minutes."

"Okay, Mom," Reggie and I replied in unison.

Briggete was on the dining room floor playing with a doll.

"Hey, Brigg, we're about ready to eat. Better put your doll away," I said.

Briggete looked up smiling and nodded in the affirmative.

Reggie and I walked through the big archway into the living room, where dad was sitting in his easy chair, listening to the radio. Luke was on the floor reading a comic book.

Reggie put his hand on Dad's shoulder, and said, "How's it goin', Dad?"

Before Dad could answer, I chimed in, "Yeah, how was your day, Dad?"

"My day went pretty good. I'm a little tired, though," Dad replied. "You boys doin' okay?"

Sure, Dad, we had a real good time playin' in the College Woods today," Reggie commented.

"You boys didn't get into any trouble out there, did you?" Dad asked.

"What kind of trouble could you get into in the College Woods?" Reggie responded, as he winked at me.

"Hey, Dad, I just remembered, Mom wanted you to know that supper would be ready in a couple of minutes. Okay?" I asked.

"Don't worry," Dad replied. "I've never missed one of your Mother's home-cooked meals yet. Oh, by the way, can you two boys help me with the milk route Easter morning. There'll be a little something extra in your allowances if you do."

"Dad, you know me and Mark always help you on the holidays," Reggie answered. "Why should this holiday be any different? We like bein' with you. And about that little somethin' extra in our allowances, could we have that now? Me and Mark wanna go down town for awhile tonight; that is, if it's okay with you and Mom."

"It's a deal," Dad responded. "How's fifty cents extra apiece sound? And, Yeah, you can both go downtown tonight. I'm sure it'll be okay with your Mom, too. But remember, you gotta be home by Eleven.

"Gee, thanks, Dad," Reggie said, with a big smile. "We'll get done so fast Easter Sunday that it'll set the all-time record."

Luke looked up from the comic book and said, "Dad, when do I get to help on the milk route?"

"In a couple of years, Luke," Dad replied. "You gotta get a little bigger first."

Just then, Mom called from the kitchen, "Supper's ready."

During the meal, Mom and Dad discussed the improvements they would make on the house this summer. Mom had finally saved enough money to get the roof reshingled and have siding put on the house.

I listened half heartedly to their conversation, while I concentrated mainly on the delicious meal before me.

Even the sight of Luke straining his chewed-up potatoes through his front teeth, for my benefit, didn't deter me from the mission at hand.

After I had devoured five salmon patties, two helpings of potatoes, and my salad, I leaned back in my chair while rubbing my stomach, and asked, "What's for dessert, Mom?"

"Your Dad brought some strawberry ice cream home from the dairy, but you'll have to wait until the rest of us have finished our meals," Mom answered, showing a little agitation.

It seemed like it took Briggete forever to finish her plate. I periodically glared at her from across the table. She would smile sweetly back at me, knowing full well she controlled the situation.

The ice cream topped the meal off perfectly. I was stuffed to the point of bursting my belt.

"Mom, that was some great meal," Reggie said flatteringly."

"Well, I hope you **really** enjoyed it, 'cause now Mark and you get to clean off the table and do the dishes," Mom replied with a smile.

"But, Mom, it's a quarter-to-six already, and me and Mark hafta get cleaned up so we get downtown by seven," Reggie said pleadingly.

"Don't worry, if you hurry, you'll have plenty of time," Mom argued, as she walked toward the front room to join Dad and the other two kids.

Reggie and I began to work furiously at cleaning off the table, and putting the perishable leftovers in the refrigerator. The good table scraps were fed to our pet dog, Corky.

By 6:30, we had finished the dishes, showered, and were dressed and ready to go.

The rest of the family was all gathered around the radio in the front room. "The Lone Ranger," one of Dad's favorite evening radio shows, was just coming on the air.

As I stood in the dining room, with the front door already open, Reggie looked into the front room and said, "Bye, everybody. We'll be home by eleven."

I yelled "Bye" at about the same time.

The other family members responded with their goodbyes.

A Night on the Town

It was a perfect spring evening. The sky was clear, and the temperature was about 65 degrees. It was what the older guys with convertibles called "top-down weather."

Reggie and I would have to walk fast, if we were to cover the twelve blocks to the Harrison Theater in the next twenty-five minutes.

When we arrived at the Harrison Theater, Spike was waiting there, leisurely leaning back against the front wall. "How's it hangin', guys?" was his greeting.

"We're doin' okay," Reggie replied. "How long ya been waitin'?"

"Oh, maybe ten minutes." Spike responded. "A lot of good lookin' girls out tonight."

"Well, what are we gonna do first?" I asked enthusiastically.

"Hows 'bout goin' down to Andy's Billiard Parlor and shootin' some pool?" Reggie suggested.

"Sounds good to me," I replied.

"Me too," Spike added.

Andy's was pretty busy when we arrived. It was obvious we'd have to wait a little while for a table, so we sat down on one of the benches that lined the walls of pool-table area, and began watching some of the other games that were in progress.

The old building reeked of stale tobacco smoke, and a constant haze of smoke hung about half way down from the 12-foot ceiling.

Andy's establishment was essentially one long, narrow room, about 25 feet wide and 80 feet deep.

As you entered the building, two glass-enclosed sales counters lined the right side for 30 feet. Two cash registers resided on top of the sales counters.

One display case contained the confection items and snack-type merchandise, such as candy bars, gum, peanuts, red hots (highly spiced, dried-meat sticks), potato chips, pretzels; and one whole display case was devoted to the tobacco products—such as cigarettes, cigars, and chewing tobacco.

Four card tables lined the wall opposite the sales counters.

Although gambling was illegal, everyone knew that the red, white, and blue chips that adorned the gaming tables were backed with hard cash.

The rear two-thirds of the building accommodated one snooker table and four standard pool tables.

A pair of naked fluorescent lights provided the illumination over each table.

Spittoons were strategically placed throughout the establishment.

Probably one of the most unusual sights in Andy's were the two open urinals, which were located side by side and attached to a wall in the pool area, only eight to ten feet beyond the sales counter.

As for privacy during the act of urination, the bare minimum was provided. Three 3-foot shields were mounted perpendicularly to the wall, one on the outer side of each urinal and one that formed a divider between the urinals.

From inside the building, only the back side of the urinal users was exposed. However, anyone passing in front of the pool hall, on the sidewalk outside, got full view of the users' head and shoulders protruding above the shields. From the view outside, it was not difficult to determine what kind of business was being conducted by these guys who were standing stock-still and staring intently at the blank wall in front of them.

It was not unusual to see passersby stop, peer into the windows, and then laugh hysterically once they had confirmed their suspicions, usually when the guy stepped back to zip up his trousers.

Both Spike and I registered surprise when Reggie reached in his shirt pocket and pulled out a pack of cigarettes.

"I've been savin' these for a special occasion," Reggie said in his best impersonation of a man. "You guys wanna smoke?" he asked, as he pulled a cigarette from the pack and tapped it on the back of his hand.

"Sure," Spike replied. "We gotta fit in, don't we?"

"I'll have one too, Reg," I said.

We were all sitting there smoking, when Reggie looked at Spike with astonishment and said, "Geez, you're not even inhalin', Spike. "That's a helluva waste, ya know? Hell, you're not either, Mark. Ain't you guys learned how to inhale yet? Watch this."

Reggie took a long drag on the cigarette and blew the smoke out through his nose.

"Man, that's awesome!" Spike remarked admiringly.

"Okay, now you guys try it," Reggie said.

"You go first, Spike," I suggested.

Spike put the cigarette to his mouth and took a long pull. He immediately took on the look of someone choking to death — someone fighting for his last breath. His face turned beet-red and his eyes were bulging and watering heavily, as he began to cough violently and spew out the noxious smoke.

When he could breathe again, Spike exclaimed, "Wow, for a minute, I thought I was a goner."

Reggie, who had been laughing uncontrollably at the display, finally said, "Spike, I think you took in too much smoke for the first time. Ya gotta break into this easy-like."

I tried my first drag; just a little one. Even though it irritated my throat, I was able to stifle my cough and therefore appear more manly than Spike.

It wasn't long before Spike and I were tolerating our first cigarettes pretty well.

As we sat there smoking and talking, I noticed that Andy, the pool-hall owner, was walking toward us.

He stopped and glared down at us menacingly and said, "Hey, you boys old enough to be in here?" He then narrowed his eyes and growled, "You know, you gotta be at least fifteen or you could go to jail?"

I felt as if Andy were looking straight at me, as I gulped hard and tried to think of something to say.

Reggie quickly came to the rescue by responding, "Sure, we're all old enough. I'm sixteen and these two guys are both fifteen."

Andy looked at us suspiciously for what seemed like an eternity, and finally said gruffly, "Okay, but you better not cause any trouble in here."

As Andy walked away, Spike and I both smiled at Reggie approvingly.

Reggie, very pleased with himself, was sporting a big grin.

Number 4 table had just emptied, and it was now our turn.

The attendant standing by the table asked, "What'll it be, boys?"

"Well, with three of us playin', I guess it'll hafta be rotation," Reggie replied.

"Okay, rotation it is," the attendant acknowledged, as he placed the balls in the triangular rack. "Remember, guys, it's fifteen cents a game for three of ya."

"No sweat," Reggie responded.

"Okay, we'll lag for break," Reggie suggested. "Up and down the table once with the cue ball, and kiss off the cushion at our end. The one closest to the rail gets to break." "Got that?" Reggie asked.

"Sure, we got it, Reg," replied Spike. "Ya think we're stupid or somethin'?"

"Mark, why don't you go get us three cokes while me and Spike lag?" Reggie proposed.

"Okay, if you promise not to cheat me while I'm gone," I responded.

"Don't worry, we won't cheat ya," Reggie said reassuringly.

When I returned with the cokes, Reggie and Spike had both lagged and had made chalk marks where their balls had stopped. Reggie's mark was about three inches from the cushion; Spike's was 10 to 12 inches away.

I selected one of the few straight cue sticks that were left, and then chalked up the tip liberally. I then positioned the cue ball about three inches from rail, in preparation for my lag shot.

As I leaned over the rail to take aim at the cue ball, I became a little self-conscious of the awkward bridge I'd formed with my left hand.

"Nice and easy does it," I thought to myself. *"I just hope I don't miscue."*

I sent the ball up the table, immediately worrying that I'd shot it a little too hard. However, after slowing down on the return trip, the ball barely kissed the cushion at our end, and came to rest about one inch from the rail.

"Lucky shit," Spike said derisively.

"Lucky hell," I retorted, as I positioned myself to make the first break.

I spotted the cue ball, took aim, and sent it with considerable force toward the point ball. As the balls cracked together and then broke helter-skelter in all directions, I noticed the 15-ball heading toward the corner pocket. It teetered for an instant on the edge, and then rolled in.

"Shit-house luck," Spike mumbled.

After sinking the "15", I was left with a long shot on the 1-ball. *"Might be too much green,"* I thought to myself.

I missed the corner pocket by about an inch, and set Reggie up for a side-pocket shot.

Reggie 'canned' the "one" in the side, and gained pretty good position on the two-ball. He barely missed the corner pocket with the "two," but left Spike snookered with the two-ball hidden behind the pack of balls left over from the break.

"For Chris' sakes, did you hafta do that, Reg?" Spike complained.

As Spike walked around the table, trying to figure out how best to bank the cue ball into the "two," he was accidentally jabbed in the back with a cue stick being manipulated by one of the older guys at the next table.

Spike bristled, whirled around, and said angrily, "Hey, Shithead, watch your goddamn stick, will ya?"

The guy to whom Spike addressed the insult was probably 18 years old, maybe 6 feet tall, and about 190 pounds. His friend was a little shorter and stockier.

The big guy looked at Spike, laid his pool cue on the table, and growled, "Why you little prick! Are you tired of livin' or somethin'?"

Spike moved quickly and was up against the guy, punching his forefinger in his chest, saying, "You wanna make somethin' of it, asshole?"

The big guy fired back, "Let's step outside, piss-ant!"

Reggie, sensing big trouble, moved quickly behind Spike and grabbed his arms. With Spike immobilized, Reggie looked at the two guys and said calmly, "We don't want any trouble, fellas." "Okay?"

The shorter guy at the table next to us seemed to also understand the seriousness of the situation, when he responded by patting his friend on the shoulder and, while tugging at his arm, saying, "Come on, Jack, what would it prove?"

"I guess you're right, Bill," the big guy said resignedly. "But I'd better not hear anything else from that little fucker, or he's dead-meat."

Spike, whose face was fiery red by this time, was ready to go after the big guy, when Reggie spun him around, and snapped, "Leave it alone, Spike! We don't want any trouble with these guys. Besides, we're lucky Andy didn't hear all that shit."

Spike's hands were shaking when he took his shot, and he missed miserably.

"You gonna be okay, Spike?" I asked.

"Yeah, but I coulda whipped that guy's ass," he said, his eyes beginning to well up.

We played four games of rotation—Reggie winning two, and Spike and I winning one each—before we walked out of Andy's into the evening air.

As we walked down Marshall Street toward Main Street, Reggie commented pensively, "I gotta feelin' somethin' real bad is gonna happen tonight."

Still sporting his bruised feelings, Spike fired back sarcastically, "Because of what happened back at Andy's, I suppose."

"Hell no, it's just somethin' that's been gnawin' at me all night," Reggie replied.

The scene on Main Street was about what I had expected: older guys in cars cruising slowly up and the down the main drag; teenagers without cars, or too young to drive, walking and mingling on the sidewalks; guys in the cars yelling out the windows at the girls who were strolling up and down Main Street, while looking their sexy best; cars pulling along side the curb, with the male occupants leaning out the windows, trying desperately to make the 'pickup'; and family members trying valiantly to weave their way through the parade of teenagers, in an attempt to get in some last-minute shopping before the local merchants close their stores.

Along the way, we would meet guys our own ages whom we knew, and would stop briefly to exchange notes with them — notes such as "where the action was", who were the girls they'd seen tonight, etc. — before continuing on our aimless journey along Main Street.

Reggie was the first to see and recognize the three girls; they were about 100 feet in front of us and walking in our direction.

As the girls drew closer, Reggie nudged me with his elbow and said softly, "Those three girls comin' our way. They're all in my Freshman class at Saint Matthew's."

"You mean the redhead and the two blonds?" I inquired eagerly.

"Yeah, yeah," Reggie scolded. "Not so damn loud."

Then Spike came to life, asking excitedly, "You mean those three good-lookers passing in front of the Penney's Store? Man, that redhead's got some body."

"Yeah, that's them," Reggie replied. "Watch me make my move."

Reggie swaggered up to the girls, and in his most-practiced suave manner, said "Good evening, ladies. Would you do us the honor of joining us for sodas at Jerry's Drive Inn? The treat's on us."

The redhead, who appeared insulted by the proposal, glared at him and responded sarcastically, "Reggie Gearing, why don't you and your friends just get lost? Can't you see we're trying to get picked up by some of the older guys with cars?"

"Yeah," one of the blonds added, "Look us up when you've got a set of wheels, creeps."

Reggie, whose red face revealed his embarrassment, recovered quickly enough to retaliate with, "When I get my car, there won't be no ugly broads like you in it!" "Come on, guys, let's get out of here."

When the girls were out of earshot, Reggie looked at Spike and me and said, "Don't you guys say a damn word about this. Got it?"

Spike feigning hurt feelings looked at Reggie and said, "Gee, Reg, I wasn't gonna say anything." "You think I'm insensitive or somethin'," he continued, giving me a wink.

"Let's go down to Jerry's, anyway," I suggested. "I'm gettin' hungry."

"Heck yeah," Spike added. "There'll be a lot of kids down there."

"Okay, but I don't wanna run into those girls again," Reggie said.

We changed directions and began walking south on Main Street.

It was apparent as we crossed over the Main Street Bridge, which spanned the Wabash River, that the river was still raging from the recent rain storms. The water level was so high that it was impossible to detect the little dam just one-hundred yards east of the bridge.

As on every Friday night, the car-hops were busily attending the cars that ringed Jerry's, and the inside of the circular building was bustling with kids.

Once inside the building, we were greeted with the loud, rhythmic sounds from the juke box. The bass notes actually vibrated the windows.

The familiar, mouth-watering smell that permeated the air was from the thousands of hamburgers and french fries that had been prepared in the open cooking area, at the end of horseshoe-shaped counter.

"There's an open booth," Reggie noted. "Let's grab it."

Once in the booth, Reggie asked, "One of you guys got a nickel? "I wanna hear "Peg of My Heart."

"Sure, here, Reg," I said, as I handed him a nickel.

As Reggie placed his coin in the money slot of the juke box, Spike said excitedly, "Hey, Reg, did you see that little brunette over by the door staring at you?"

"Sure, I saw her," Reggie replied. "But she ain't my type. I personally like 'em a little more developed than that."

Just then, a very pretty waitress showed up to take our orders. "What can I do for you boys?" she asked politely.

"I can think of a number of things," Reggie quipped, with a big smile.

"The waitress, who was used to that kind of a response, said, "Let's keep this strictly business, fellas. I've got an awfully big boy friend."

"I'll bet the **awful** part fits him pretty good, anyway," Reggie responded with a grin, obviously pleased with his own cleverness.

"Okay, guys, give me your orders," she said, ignoring Reggie's last remark.

"I'll have a grilled cheese sandwich, fries, and a coke," I said.

"Make mine the same," Spike added.

"Well, if all I can have is food, make it a grilled cheese sandwich, plenty of dill pickles, and a chocolate malt," Reggie said, winking at the waitress.

"Okay, but it'll be a little while," she said, as she smiled and walked away.

"Listen, here comes my song," Reggie said. "I really like this by the Mills Brothers."

We all listened intently during Reggie's selection.

When the song had ended, Spike expressed his pleasure by stating, "I gotta agree with ya, Reg, them guys can really sing."

We talked idly for another ten minutes before the waitress showed up with the food.

It didn't take us long to polish off our goodies.

I looked at my watch and was surprised to see that it was already ten o'clock. "Hey, fellas, we'd better wrap this up, if Reg and me are gonna be home by eleven, like we promised," I noted.

We all chipped in to leave the waitress a 25-cent tip, and then proceeded to the cashier to pay our checks.

Once we left Jerry's, we headed north on Main Street. The traffic on Main Street was beginning to thin out.

We crossed the bridge and then the Wabash Railroad tracks, and continued on past the front of the old courthouse. Two blocks north of the courthouse, we turned right (east) on Marshall Street, and began our walk that would take us by Andy's and several bars that lined the south side of the street.

By taking this route, Reggie and I could walk Spike to his house on Frost Street and then continue on to our home, without having gone very far out of our way.

We had just progressed a half-block and were crossing the entrance to the first alleyway, which was sandwiched between two bars on Marshall Street, when we heard noises emanating from somewhere deep in the alley.

We stopped and stared hard into the dimly lit corridor. We could hear loud, angry voices and could make out two vague figures moving about in the small parking area behind the Shamrock Bar.

As we strained to see more clearly, the scene began to come into focus.

Chris', it looks like some huge guy and a sailor are fightin' back there," Reggie said in a shaky voice. "My God, the big guy's got a knife! We gotta do somethin' quick!"

"I'll run in the bar an get some help," I said nervously.

"Forget that. There ain't time," Reggie fired back. "We're gonna hafta do somethin' ourselves."

We began moving stealthily toward the melee, staying close up against the building to take full advantage of the concealment provided by the shadows. At times we could see the glint from the knife, as the hulking figure lunged at the sailor.

The sailor, who we could see more clearly now, was in full dress-blue uniform except for his white hat. He was jumping quickly from side to side, trying desperately to avoid the deadly blade. Each time the knife passed close to his body, the sailor would try to grab the right arm of his knife-wielding adversary.

The big man, who had just made a forward thrust and missed, was off balance for a moment. Capitalizing on his momentary advantage, the sailor crashed his right fist hard into the bigger man's face.

The larger man, who looked to be at least six-foot four and 300 pounds or more, bellowed in pain as the blood spurted from his mouth. As he staggered backward, he cursed loudly, "You're gonna die for that, you son-of-a-bitch!"

Reggie raised his hand signaling us to stop, and whispered, "I'm gonna go for his right arm. Mark you get the left one, and, Spike, you take his feet out from under him."

We had just started moving forward again, when we saw the two figures come together. The sailor groaned and fell backward in a sitting position, holding his side. The big man's knife had found its mark.

We were now coming up fast from behind, as the hulking brute moved in for the kill. Reggie was there first and grabbed the guy's right arm, the one wielding the knife. I was barely able to grab the left arm, as he tugged hard to break Reggie's grip.

The man was so strong that he actually pulled us off our feet and began swinging us in a circle, howling obscenities as he tried to shake free.

I held on for dear life, all the time thinking, *"Where in the hell is Spike?" "I can't hold on much longer."*

All of a sudden, Spike was in front us, diving for the guy's feet.

With perfect timing, the big guy drop-kicked Spike square in face. The force of the kick lifted Spike's entire body up and propelled him backward for several feet, where he landed in a lifeless heap.

"Okay, now I'll take care of you little bastards," the big man growled, as he continued to swing Reggie and me around, in an attempt to free his arms.

As we were being swung wildly about, Reggie and I wrapped our legs around those of the big guy, in an attempt to make him lose his balance. All this did was make him curse louder.

At one point during the struggle, the big guy used all the force he could muster to fling me, while I still clung tightly to his massive left arm, into the rear wall of the Shamrock Bar. My head hit the bricks hard, but I didn't release my grip. It left me groggy and weak, and I could feel the warm blood streaming down the left side of my face. Blackness was beginning to overcome me.

"This is it," I thought. *"This is where Reg and I die."*

I heard the "thud" and felt the impact that caused the big guy to lurch forward and then go limp, dragging Reggie and me to the ground with him.

As Reggie and I wriggled free and got to our feet, there was Spike standing in front us, still clutching the piece of two-by-four in his hands and trying to manage a smile through his broken and bloody lips.

"Who was that masked man?" Spike joked.

For the first time, I was aware of the soft sobbing sounds coming from a darkened corner, formed by the junction of two buildings. We walked cautiously toward the sound and were shocked to find a beautiful dark-haired girl cowering in the corner.

"It's okay now, lady," Reggie said reassuringly, as he reached out his hand to help her up. "Nobody's gonna hurt you."

"Is that your boyfriend over there?" Reggie asked, pointing to the sailor, who was still in a sitting position, groaning, and holding his side.

"Yes, that's Jimmy Cartwright…he's my fiancé," she replied softly. "Thank you very much for your help," she said gratefully. She was showing a faint smile, as she began using her handkerchief to wipe away the tears.

Reggie, who was leaning over the sailor to get a closer look, pronounced somberly, "This guy may be hurt pretty bad. We gotta get him some help."

The sailor uttered his first words: "Thanks, fellas, but I think I'll be okay. This whole thing got started because that big, drunk son-of-a - bitch made a pass at Millie in the bar. The most important thing now is that I get back to Great Lakes by 6:00 tomorrow morning, when my leave is up."

"Let's worry first about how bad ya been cut," Reg said, as he pulled up the sailor's jumper to inspect his wound.

The puncture wound was bleeding badly, but it was off to the side far enough to have missed vital organs. The palms of the sailor's hands were also badly lacerated from his attempts to grab the knife.

The big man on the ground was moaning now and beginning to move slightly.

"We better get our asses outta here," Reggie said, the urgency showing in his voice.

"I've got my car parked down by the courthouse. Can you guys help us get to it?" the sailor asked.

"No sweat, "Reggie replied.

It turned out that the sailor and his girlfriend were both from Harrington. Millie Waverly was a Senior at Harrington High, and Jimmy, who had been in the Navy for two years, had graduated from Harrington High three years earlier.

Reggie and I, each holding onto an arm, were able to support Jimmy's 180 pounds easily at first. We had only to walk down the alley for a half a block to get to the north side of the courthouse.

Spike and the girl walked a few feet behind us. Reggie and I shuffled along with Jimmy suspended between us. By this time Jimmy, who was weakening fast, had an arm draped over each of our shoulders. At times, he could not lift his feet, causing the toes of his shoes to drag along noisily on the brick surface of the alley.

Jimmy's dead weight was beginning to take its toll. Reggie and I were panting breathlessly when we finally arrived at our destination on the east side of the courthouse, where the black 1937 Chevrolet was parked.

Looking at Reggie, the sailor said, "My car keys, they're in my jumper pocket."

Without a word, Reggie got the keys and unlocked the driver's side door, while I continued to prop up the sailor.

"Put me behind the wheel, will ya?" Jimmy asked weakly.

"Jimmy, you're in no condition to drive!" the girl snapped. "Let one of the boys drive us to a place where we can get some help," she stated, in a surprisingly commanding voice.

"Okay, Honey, I guess you're right," Jimmy replied meekly. "Can any of you guys drive?" Jimmy asked, looking at each of us. "Millie hasn't learned how yet. I was gonna teach her this summer."

"Sure," Reggie replied, "I can drive. I learned to drive my Dad's car, a '37 Chevy, just like this one. Problem is, I ain't got a driver's license yet."

"We'll just have to take that chance," Jimmy replied. "Put me in the back seat so Millie can work on my cuts."

With great effort, Reggie and I helped Jimmy into the back seat, directly behind the driver's seat.

"Would one of you boys open my trunk and get some of my clean skivvy shirts out of my sea bag?" Jimmy asked. "We can tear 'em up for bandages," he explained.

Spike took the keys and headed for the trunk. Reggie got in behind the wheel, and I went to the opposite side of the car and climbed in the front seat with him.

We heard the trunk lid slam shut, and almost immediately Spike was sliding into the front seat, pushing me to the center.

"Ya think four is enough?" Spike asked, as he passed the shirts back to Millie.

"I'm sure four will be plenty," Millie replied.

She handed Spike back one the shirts and said, "Please take this one into the courthouse restroom and soak it good with water? I'll need it to clean Jimmy's wounds," she explained.

"I'll be right back," Spike said, as he took off at a dead run.

"You really should see a doctor, Jimmy," Millie pleaded.

"I'll be okay, Hon," Jimmy told her confidently. "Besides, it's after eleven now, and I gotta cover over 200 miles in the next six hours or so."

Spike arrived with the wet shirt and passed it back to Millie, as he slid in beside me.

As Millie began washing Jimmy's wounds, she said, "It just dawned on me…You boys have done so much for us, and we don't even know your names yet."

The three of us introduced ourselves to Millie and Jimmy.

"Jimmy, I think the bleeding has stopped," Millie observed. "But you're still in no condition to drive back to the base. Is there anyway you boys could make the trip with us?" she pleaded.

Spike answered first, "No problem for me. My Dad's out on a train run until tomorrow afternoon, and my Mom's in Logansport helpin' my older sister have her baby. Mom won't be home till tomorrow night."

"And I can call my Mom and Dad and tell 'em that me and Mark are stayin' all night with Spike," Reggie added excitedly.

"Gee, that's great, fellas," Millie said appreciatively. "And after we drop Jimmy off at the Navy Base, I'll be coming back to Harrington with you."

"Reggie, don't you think you should make that phone call now?" she asked.

Reggie replied, "Yeah, there's a phone booth at the filling station across the street. I'll be right back."

Millie continued bandaging Jimmy's wounds, as we waited for Reggie to return.

It was no more than three minutes before Reggie was sliding behind the steering wheel again.

"Did you have any trouble gettin' permission to stay at Spike's tonight?" I inquired.

"Well, for a minute it was 'touch and go', Reggie explained. I woke Dad up, and you gotta know that didn't make 'im too happy." "The first thing he said was: "Ya know, it's almost eleven-thirty. Why the hell did ya wait so long to call?"

He sounded real pissed off, so I said, "Gee, Dad, we were lookin' all over downtown for a public phone to use. I guess the time just got away from us." "He musta bought it," Reggie continued, 'cause he finally said: "Well, okay, but be home by noon tomorrow.""

By this time, Millie had finished cleaning and dressing Jimmy's wounds.

Jimmy seemed to be feeling better as he said, "I think I'll ride up front with Reggie, so I can show him the way. Mark, you and Spike get in the back with Millie. That'll give me a little room to stretch in the front seat."

Jimmy was able to move out of the car and into the front seat without assistance. His improvement over the last half an hour seemed truly remarkable. However, he readily admitted that his hands were way too sore to grasp the steering wheel.

Millie sat in the middle of the back seat, with Spike and I on either side. I was positioned behind the driver's seat, where Reggie sat.

As Reggie eased the Chevy away from the curb, he glanced into the rear-view mirror and exclaimed, "Oh shit, there's a cop car comin' up behind. They're probably lookin' around on accounta that fight."

"Just keep drivin' like nothin's wrong, and we'll be okay," Jimmy said with an easy manner, trying to calm Reggie.

Reggie made his 5-foot-ten, 145-pound frame look as big as he could in the driver's seat. Once out in the street, he began driving slowly south on Harding Street. The squad car was now following about four car lengths behind the Chevy.

"Don't drive too slow, Reg. It'll look suspicious," Jimmy warned. "Turn left at Court Street, and see if they follow."

"Okay," Reggie answered, his voice betraying his nervousness.

Reggie set his turn signal and turned onto Court Street.

"Geez, they're gonna turn too," he said in a shaky voice.

"Don't worry, Reg. They just like to rattle people," Jimmy said reassuringly. "Just turn left on Frost Street, and we'll keep right on goin' out of town on U.S. 24."

The police car followed us all the way to the Harrington city limits sign, where it made a U-turn and headed back to town.

"See, what did I tell ya?" Jimmy boasted. "They used to follow me all the time when I was learnin' to drive".

"Well, I'm glad it's over, anyway. They had me pretty worried for awhile," Reggie said gratefully.

"Turn north on Highway 9," Jimmy instructed. "We'll pick up 30 at Colscott City. That'll take us right into Chicago."

"You mean I gotta drive through Chicago?" Reggie asked in amazement.

"No problem," Jimmy replied. "All you gotta do is keep up with the traffic on Northshore Drive."

"Jimmy, whadda ya do in the Navy?" Reggie asked.

"Well, I'm an instructor at the Radioman School. Outta Boot Camp, I wanted to get a ship and go to sea and see some action, but it looks like I'm gonna be stuck at Great Lakes for at least the rest of the year," Jimmy explained.

"Yeah, I guess goin' to sea is what bein' in the Navy is all about," Reggie acknowledged.

In the back seat, Millie turned to me and said, "Mark, let me see if I can do something for that cut on your head. I still have a clean piece of that damp undershirt left." "Lay your head here," she said, as she pulled the right side of my face to her bosom."

My heart was racing rapidly as my face met with the softness of her breast. Her beautiful blue eyes seemed to penetrate my soul as she bent over me and applied the cool fabric softly to my cheek. The sweet, clean fragrance of her body overwhelmed me…It was as if we were one.

"Does that hurt, Mark?" She asked tenderly, as she began to wash my cut in a soft stroking motion.

"Oh no, it feels really good, Millie," I replied appreciatively.

Her touch was so soothing that I soon fell asleep with my head still resting against her body. Beautiful dreams flooded my mind.

She allowed me to stay there until I awoke.

I awoke with a start, almost a half an hour later, and said in a surprised voice, "Oh, I'm sorry, Millie, I didn't mean to fall asleep."

"Well, it's understandable that you'd be tired after what you've been through tonight," she said graciously. "You know, you were pretty heroic tonight."

"Aw, it wasn't nothin'," I said as I sat up, my face feeling hot from the moment of embarrassment. She would never know how I felt about her at that moment.

"Where are we now?" I asked, attempting to change the subject.

"Well, we passed through Colscott City a little while ago. We're now on U.S. 30, about 150 miles from Chicago," Millie replied.

Feeling a little self-conscious, I looked over at Spike to see if he had seen anything. His head was resting against the window, and he was snoring softly.

Jimmy was asleep in the front.

I leaned forward and tapped Reggie on the shoulder. "Are you gettin' sleepy yet, Reg?" I asked.

"Naw, gettin' to do all this drivin' has been too much fun to think about sleepin'," Reggie replied. "I can always sleep. Besides, this hot music on the radio helps keep me awake."

Jimmy awoke as we neared Valparaiso, Indiana. "Hey, Reg, we need to stop pretty soon for gas and somethin' to eat," Jimmy noted. "I know a good truck stop right outside of Valpo. I'll even pick up the tab for the chow, to show you guys my appreciation for what you did for Millie and me tonight."

"That ain't necessary, Jimmy," Reggie countered.

"I wanna do it, and that's all there is to it," Jimmy insisted.

When we stopped at the truck stop, Jimmy opened his trunk and took out a clean skivvy shirt, a jumper, and a white hat from his sea bag. We all took turns freshening up in the restroom, before we went into the restaurant.

While we were waiting for our meals, Jimmy said to Reggie, "After you drop me off at Great Lakes and drive back to Harrington, you can leave my car at Millie's house. I'll be back in Harrington next weekend. I got a 8-hour leave comin'."

"Sure thing, Jimmy," Reggie responded.

"Another thing," Jimmy continued, I don't want anybody worryin' about my cuts. "I gotta buddy whose a Corpsman Second Class. He can clean me up, and do some stichin' where it's needed. I'll be in fine shape."

We all ate heartily, while we engaged in small talk.

The rest of the trip was uneventful. We had Jimmy back at Great Lakes at 5:30, with a half an hour to spare.

Jimmy gave Millie a long kiss before he exited the car, and starting walking, with his sea bag on his shoulder, to the main gate of the navy base. As we were about to drive away, he turned and yelled, "See you next Friday night, Hon…. and thanks a million, guys."

We all waved good-bye to Jimmy, and Reggie turned the old Chevy toward home.

We arrived back in Harrington at 9:55.

Our first stop was Spike's house. As Spike was leaving the car, Reggie said, "We'll see you Monday morning. Me and Mark are gonna go with my dad on his milk route tomorrow, and I'm sure we'll hafta stay home tonight and get some sleep."

"Okay, I'll see you guys Monday," Spike replied. "I think I'll stay home tonight and get some sack time too."

Next, we drove to Millie's house, where we bid her good-bye and left the car parked the in her driveway.

Reggie and I walked home from Millie's house.

When we walked into the house about 10:30, Mom noticed immediately the cut and swelling on the left side of my head. "What in the world happened to your head, Mark?" she said, concern showing in her voice.

"It's nothin', Mom," I replied nonchalantly. "Us guys were rough-housin' in Spike's bed last night, and I rolled out and cracked my head. It don't hurt much." " Is it okay if Reg and me eat a little somethin' and then go to bed for awhile? We were messin' around most of the night at Spike's house and didn't get much sleep."

"Yes, but you'll have to help me for about an hour," she replied. "We still have a couple of things to do, so the house will be just right for Easter Sunday."

Neither Reggie nor I felt much like doing chores at this time, but we felt almost obligated, because of the things we'd done the night before — and had apparently gotten away with.

We crashed in our beds about 1:00 in the afternoon, and slept through the rest of the afternoon and all the way through the night.

Dad called us for church at 4:00 o'clock Easter morning. The entire Gearing family attended the 5:00 o'clock Sunrise Mass at Saint Matthews. After mass, we came home and had a quick breakfast. Dad, Reggie, and I then changed into our work clothes.

While we were walking to the garage to get the car, Dad looked at Reggie, and, waving the car keys tauntingly, said, "Hey, Reg, how would you like to drive the Chevy down to the dairy?"

Reggie, feigning sheer delight, said," Oh Gee, Dad, could I, really?"

"Sure, here's the keys," Dad replied, as he tossed them to Reggie.

When we arrived at the dairy, Reggie parked the car very expertly behind the building. Once out of the car, he handed the keys to Dad, and we began walking to the big garage, which housed the milk truck.

On the way to the garage, Dad had a look of bewilderment, as he said to Reggie, "Son, I can't believe how well you're drivin' now. You seem to handle the gear shift and clutch perfectly. All your turns and stops are also much better. That's amazing for no more than you get to drive. I just don't understand it."

"Yeah, Dad, it does seem like I'm gettin' a lot better at drivin'. It must be 'cause I practice it in my mind all the time," Reggie said, as he looked at me with a devilish grin on his face.

We did made our record milk-route run that day, just as we'd hoped. We were back home at 12:30 PM, the earliest ever for a holiday. Awaiting us was a scrumptious Easter dinner, consisting of roast turkey with all the trimmings, sweet potatoes, corn, green bean casserole, scalloped potatoes, and homemade dinner rolls — and to top it all off, homemade pumpkin pie with lots of whipped cream. Certainly a feast to remember!

Boxcars and Home Brew

Monday morning dawned bright and clear — a perfect day for some outdoor activities.

Reggie and I slept until 9:00 in the morning, when Mom called from the bottom of the stairway that it was time to get up. Not often were we allowed to stay in bed this late, so we took full advantage of it.

Mom had a breakfast of bacon and eggs ready for us when we came downstairs.

Dad had gone to work over four hours earlier. Luke was already outside playing with some of the neighbor boys his own age. Briggete was walking around the house giggling, wearing one of Mom's Sunday hats and a pair of her high-heel shoes.

As Reggie and I began eating, Mom said, "All you boys have to do is clean up the dirty dishes, then you can get together with your friends."

When we had finished our breakfast, Reggie said, "Mark, why don't you start washin' the dishes while I call up the other guys?"

"Okay, but you're not gonna trick me into doin' the whole job," I replied emphatically.

In about ten minutes, Reggie was back in the kitchen saying, "The guys will all be here by 10:00. Since you're about done washin' 'em, why don't you help me dry 'em, so we can be all done by the time the other guys get here?"

Although his request seemed logical at the time, I couldn't help feeling I was being 'had'. Finally, without a word, I reluctantly grabbed a dish towel and began helping him.

Pete arrived first, at about 9:45. Mom met him at the door and invited him inside.

I glanced into the dining room to say hello to Pete, and he had already made it to the front room, where he was sitting on the sofa, reading a comic book.

"Hey, Pete, we're just wrappin' up the dishes," I yelled. "We'll be with ya in a couple a minutes."

Without looking up from the comic book, Pete replied, "That's okay, the other guys ain't even here yet."

A couple of minutes later, Reggie and I joined Pete in the front room.

"Let's go out on the front porch and wait for the other guys," Reggie suggested. "It's too nice a day to be sittin' in here."

"Geez, Reg, I'm just to the good part. Batman's beatin' the hell outta the bad guy," Pete complained.

"Don't sweat it." Reggie responded. "You can take it home later and finish it."

The three of us were sitting on the front porch steps, enjoying the bright sunshine, when Dan and Wally arrived.

We could see Spike walking up Finley Street.

"As we all stood on the front lawn, Pete inquired, "Did you guys have fun Friday night?"

"Yeah, I'd say we had us a little fun," Reggie replied, with a grin. "What would you say, Spike?"

"Yeah, I guess we had some interesting things happen," Spike said, smiling slyly.

"Too bad the rest of you guys couldn't a been with us," I added, as I winked at Spike.

"Well, c'mon, let's hear about it," Wally said impatiently.

We all sat on the porch steps as Reggie, standing in front of us, narrated the whole story. From time to time, Spike and I jumped in with our own comments, to further embellish the story.

When Reggie had finished relating all the events of Friday night and Saturday morning, there was a long silence.

Pete was the first to speak, "You made up all that shit, right, Reg?"

"Yeah, you know you can go to hell for lyin'," Dan added, with a sarcastic smile.

"You don't expect us to believe that bull shit, do you?" Wally said, shaking his head. "The way you guys can make up stories, you oughta be writin' books."

"I just might do that someday," I said jokingly.

"Well, fellas, I know it's hard to believe that three of your best buddies are genuine heroes, but it's true," Reggie said smugly. "Maybe if I introduce you to Millie sometime, you'll believe me."

"Whadda we gonna do today?" Dan asked.

"Let's go down by the Harrington Labs and check out the creek," Reggie suggested. "Maybe the water level's dropped enough so we can do some more explorin' on the inside of the old sewer tunnel."

The College Woods creek flowed directly into the main conduit of the Harrington sewer system, which we called "the tunnel." A four-foot, concrete step formation had been constructed across the creek bed, about 200 feet from the tunnel entrance. The sudden drop in the creek bed elevation accelerated the water speed, thus providing the natural flushing action needed to move along the contents of the tunnel.

The tunnel itself was a 12-foot diameter, brick-lined tube that ran underground for about two miles in a south-westerly direction, before it emptied into the Wabash River.

Many smaller, 4-foot, concrete sewer pipes dumped into the tunnel all along its course to the river. The smaller pipes generally intersected the brick-lined curve of the tunnel at a height of about five feet above its base.

Like all old sewer systems, the tunnel carried away rain water, household waste water, human waste, and anything else that people decided to flush down their toilets. The brick walls were slick and slimy from all the waste materials that had poured into the tunnel from the smaller arteries.

When the creek was flowing normally, no more than a foot of water ran along the bottom of the tunnel. It was during these periods in the past that we were able to crawl down the limestone walls that lined the creek, and then enter the tunnel by stepping from the limestone to the brick interior.

Once inside the tunnel, in order to move forward, one had to run from one side of the curved brick wall to the other, in a zigzag fashion, while jumping over the three-foot wide stream each time. The biggest threat we faced, while performing this maneuver, was the potential for slipping on the slick bricks and falling into the putrid stream that ran beneath us — for in that stream was a concoction of unknown chemicals from the Harrington Labs and all the human waste products collected from a countless number of Harrington households.

The seemingly potent mixture, however, proved to be somewhat less deadly than we had once feared, because, at one time or another, we had each accidentally fallen into the smelly slime and survived.

One other thing that added excitement to the experience were the huge, black sewer rats that scurried about as we humans invaded their subterranean domain.

The first part of the tunnel ran directly under Highway U.S. 24. In fact, when you passed under the highway, you could here the cars running overhead.

About 100 feet from the entrance, the tunnel began turning to the right. Another 100 feet and the light became non-existent. That is when you could no longer see the rats, but you could feel them run across your feet.

The only real deadly aspect of a tunnel trip was the sewer gas that one encountered deep in the bowels of the tunnel. For this reason, we never ventured more than about a thousand feet inside.

Pete Rocelli's dad, Joe, told the story of how he and another policeman, along with some of the local firemen, made an inspection tour of the complete length of the big tunnel. Joe said they had to don their gas masks before they had progressed even half way through the system. By the time they had put on their gas masks, two of the men had passed out, and later, outside the tunnel, became violently ill and had to be taken to the hospital for treatment.

Our trip of about three city blocks to the creek took us first to the end of Kimmel Street, where we cut between two houses that fronted Campfield Street. We then passed through the wooded area that lined the back yards of the two houses; then over and down the hill, which passed behind the Harrington Labs. The creek was only about 200 feet east of the Labs' main building.

When we reached the banks of the creek, our spirits sagged. The water had receded significantly from what we had seen the previous Friday, but it was still too high to allow a front-entrance into the tunnel.

"Well, I guess this about kills the tunnel idea," Reggie said matter-of-factly."

"No, wait a minute. I got another idea," Spike said eagerly. "Across 24, on the other side of the Erie viaduct, there's one of the smaller sewer pipes that I think runs into the tunnel. Let's check it out."

"Whadda we got to lose?" Reggie responded approvingly.

Spike led the way across 24 to the grassy field. We then walked a short distance to the viaduct structure, which elevated the Erie Railroad tracks above the highway. After passing under the huge archway that was formed by the concrete underpinnings on the right side of the viaduct, we proceeded another 100 feet, to the spot where we found the opening to the 4-foot drain pipe.

The drain pipe, which was located at the end of a ditch, was obviously there for the purpose of removing storm water. As Spike had speculated, the pipe appeared to be running toward the big tunnel.

Since no one readily volunteered to lead the way through the pipe, Reggie suggested that we 'draw sticks' — the guy choosing the shortest one would lead the way.

Reggie, using twigs he had found under a nearby tree, conducted the drawing.

When we presented our sticks, Wally had the shortest. I would be second; Reggie third; Dan fourth: Pete fifth; and Spike would bring up the rear.

Needless to say, Wally was not too happy with his placement.

"Well, it looks like ol' Wally gets screwed again," he whined, as the rest of us broke into laughter.

In order to move inside the 4-foot pipe, we had to bend our knees slightly and hunch our upper bodies forward. At least, there was no water to contend with.

As Wally moved slowly forward, I held on to the back part his belt with my right hand. Reggie held onto my belt; Dan held onto Reggie's, and so on.

The prolonged right-hand curve of the pipe caused the light at our backs to vanish within the first hundred feet. Another fifty feet and we were in total blackness.

Wally, beginning to slow down noticeably, turned his head and said nervously, "Geez, fellas, I can't see nothin'. What if I step on a rat or somethin'? Somebody else wanna trade places with me?"

From the rear, Spike yelled, "C'mon, You chicken-shit. Get your ass movin'."

Our human train began shuffling slowly forward again.

We had probably progressed about 300 feet into the pipe, when Reggie exclaimed, "Damn, it's really beginnin' to stink in here! If any-body starts gettin' dizzy, we'd better turn around and get outta here in a hurry."

"Yeah, I smell it too," Spike noted. "It's really strong back here."

At that moment, Spike could feel Pete's belt heaving convulsively, and could hear his muffled giggles.

"Goddamit, Pete, it was you, wasn't it?" Spike yelled accusingly. "You sonnuvabitch! You farted right in my face! Man, them Italian spaghetti farts could wipe outta army."

Pete collapsed to his knees, cackling hysterically, too weak to stand.

Just then, Reggie began his vocal rendition of the *William Tell's Overture:* Ta-dum, Ta-dum, Ta-dum-dum-dum — Ta-dum, Ta-dum, Ta-dum-dum-dum…" Wally, Dan, and I chimed in, picking up on the rhythm. As the three of us provided the background music, Reggie began reciting those now famous words: "From out the past comes the thundering hoof beats of the great horse Silver…The Lone Ranger rides again."

As we all roared with laughter, Spike screamed, "C'mon, guys, gimme a break, will ya?"

Once our moment of frivolity had subsided, we continued our trek into the unknown.

It seemed as if we'd been in the sewer pipe forever, and the small of my back was beginning to ache badly from being hunched over for so long. I frantically wanted to see light and to be able to stand upright again.

I think by this time we were all feeling some degree of claustrophobia.

The silence was broken when Wally screamed hysterically, "I gotta get the hell outta here…I can't take it any longer!"

His sudden outburst sent cold chills up my back.

I jerked on his belt and said as calmly as I could, "For Chris' sakes, Wally, take it easy. We shouldn't have much farther to go."

We moved forward some more, and I had just begun to feel a blast of cool air on my face, when suddenly Wally seemed to drop away into the black void in front of us. He screamed as he fell, pulling me along with him as I clung tightly to his belt.

"What the hell's goin' on up there!" yelled Spike.

My forward motion finally stopped at the very end of the drain pipe. I had skidded the last few feet on my knees, still holding onto Wally's belt with a virtual death-grip. I found myself bent acutely forward by Wally's weight, as he hung suspended a few feet above the stream of liquid waste that ran beneath him. We had reached the big tunnel.

"Don't drop me!" Wally pleaded.

Reggie tugged on my belt to assist me in pulling Wally back up into the smaller pipe. Just when it seemed we were beginning to make progress, Wally's belt parted, and he plunged face first into the 3-foot deep stream below.

Wally came up spitting and coughing, and yelling hysterically, "Oh my God, I think I swallowed some of that stuff!"

Reggie and I together, while leaning out of the little pipe, were able to pull Wally back up into the drain pipe.

No one really laughed at Wally this time. I think we each put ourselves in his place, and concluded that, were it not for the luck of the draw, one of us could have taken the plunge instead of him. However, that's where our empathy ended; once we had made our return trip and were out of the drain pipe again, we were careful not get too close to Wally, who had begun to smell a little pungent by this time.

As we walked back in the direction of the Harrington Labs, Spike began to taunt Wally by saying, "Hey, Wally, could you walk a little downwind from the rest of us? You're beginning to get a little ripe."

Reggie interrupted Spike's frivolous endeavor, by saying, "C'mon, Spike, give the poor guy a break. Don't you think he's been punished enough?"

Spike flashed a mean look at Reggie, but didn't say anything.

We were walking along the path next to the creek, when Dan yelled, "Hey, fellas, there's a boxcar sittin' on the Harrington Labs' track...Let's check it out."

We immediately changed our direction and began walking across the field, toward the boxcar.

The boxcar sat on the spur line that ran diagonally from the main Erie tracks to the big loading dock, on the north side of the Labs' main building. The spur line ran downhill, at a moderately steep grade, from the main track. A 12-foot diameter, 50-foot long concrete culvert provided the means for the spur line to bridge the College Woods creek.

Once we reached the big, red boxcar — which was parked approximately 400 feet from the chain-link fence that surrounded the Labs' loading/unloading compound — the six of us swarmed over it to see what hidden mysteries it had to offer.

Reggie peered inside the open sliding door and said, "This baby's empty now, but it'll probably be used later to ship some of the cleaning stuff that they make here at the Labs. I got an idea. Me and Mark'ull get inside, and the rest of you guys play like train robbers and try to get the gold we're guardin'. It'll be a little like *King of the Hill*, 'cause we'll try to push you off before you can get inside. If somebody manages to get inside and can get all the way to the end of the boxcar, where the strong box is, then two other guys get to replace us as guards, okay?"

Pete, Spike, Wally, and Dan all voiced their approval.

Reggie and I climbed up inside and positioned ourselves at opposite sides of the open doorway, ready for action.

Spike charged the door first, and had one leg up on the floor and was pulling himself inside, when Reggie arrived and administered a mighty shove. Spike fell backwards and landed on the seat of his pants, on the cinder-covered walkway that ran along the track.

Almost immediately, Pete and Dan were climbing up on opposite sides of the door opening. Reggie pushed Pete away. Dan, who I had confronted, grabbed me around the ankles and pulled, causing me to land on my rear end with my feet dangling outside.

The next thing I knew, Dan and Pete each had a hold of one of my feet and were tugging hard, trying to pull me outside. I held tightly to the edge of the doorway, while trying to jerk my feet away. As they pulled in unison against my desperate handhold on the outer edge of the doorway, my body was raised to a horizontal position and stretched taut. My fingers were beginning to pull apart, and I could visualize myself flying outside, as if shot from a giant sling shot.

Reggie arrived in the nick of time and had both arms around my chest, trying mightily to pull me back inside. A real tug-of-war ensued, my body acting as the 'rope' in the contest.

With one gigantic tug, Reggie managed to pull most of my body back inside, at the same time enabling me to free one of my legs.

I was kicking to free my right foot from Pete's grasp, when Reggie abandoned me, in order to thwart Wally's attempt to board the boxcar on the other side of the door opening.

Wally was beginning to stand up on the door sill, when Reggie drove his full weight shoulder-first into Wally's chest. Wally flew backwards as if he'd been shot from a cannon and landed on the inclined rock embankment, about five feet from the boxcar.

As Wally lay on the ground moaning and trying to catch his breath, Dan yelled, "Time out, guys, I gotta check on Wally."

All the activity was suspended while Dan helped Wally to his feet.

"Ya okay?" Dan asked.

Wally stood on unsteady legs and, while brushing the dust from his jeans, replied pitifully, "Yeah, I think so, but I don't wanna play this stupid game no more. You guys can finish it without me. I'm gonna get up on top of the boxcar."

Wally turned and started walking toward the end of the boxcar, where the vertical ladder was located.

The rest of us had begun to battle again, when Reggie, a look of shock spreading across his face, shouted from his perch in the doorway, "Hey wait a minute…Is this thing movin'?

Spike immediately looked up at Wally, who was now on top of box-car and in the process of turning the spoked, metal wheel, which was mounted near the top of the ladder. "What the hell are you doin' with that wheel," Spike demanded.

"I'm just actin' like I'm steerin' the train. That's all," Wally replied plaintively.

"Well, you'd better get your ass down in a hurry. You've just released the brake on this goddamn thing!" Spike screamed.

The boxcar was beginning to gain momentum on its run toward the main building of the Harrington Labs.

Wally, whose face had turned ashen, clambered down the ladder to safety. Reggie and I leaped out of the boxcar and onto the cinder walkway below.

Pandemonium reigned. Pete, Dan, and Spike were in front of the boxcar, trying desperately with outstretched arms to stop its forward movement. Reggie and I each had an arm hooked in the doorway, and were being pulled along.

The boxcar had now reached its full momentum. The three guys in front were forced to jump sideways, out of its path, in order to avoid being pulled under the wheels.

Reggie and I had to leave go of the sides, because the boxcar had speeded up to the point that we could no longer keep up.

We stood helplessly along the sides of the tracks as we watched the boxcar speeding toward its inevitable rendezvous with the Labs' main building.

Out of nowhere, Wally appeared. He was running alongside the boxcar, with what appeared to be a large piece of two-by-four lumber tucked under one arm. Running at full speed, he was able to pass the front of the boxcar. When he had reached a point about 15 feet in front of the boxcar, he quickly laid his piece of lumber on the track, where the right-front wheel would pass.

The front wheel of the boxcar hit the wood with splintering force, slicing through it like butter and sending the two pieces sailing away in opposite directions. The boxcar had not been slowed at all, and was now bearing down on the chain-link fence, which stood only 200 feet away.

With a look of total bewilderment, Wally cried out, "Boy, we're in deep shit now. What are we gonna do?"

The rest of us were standing there, frozen in our footsteps, when Reggie yelled, "Let's get the hell outta here! There's nothin' we can do to stop it now. Everybody split up and get outta sight. We'll meet back at our house in about 15 minutes."

Everyone began to run in blind panic.

Reggie and I ran for the cover of the College Woods. A couple of the other guys cut out for the wooded area along the creek. Two of the others sped up the hill toward Campfield Street.

Everything seemed to blur, as Reggie and I ran wildly through the trees and underbrush — tree limbs slapping our faces and thorns tearing at our flesh and clothing. As we were splashing recklessly through the swampy area, we heard the thunderous crash. My heart seem to leap from my chest, as I visualized the boxcar tearing its way through the building, workmen scurrying for their lives.

The horrifying crash spurred us to run even faster and seek sanctuary deeper into the woods.

We had reached Suicide Hill, when Reggie grabbed my arm and said breathlessly, "Let's wait here until things have had time to cool down."

We sat down, and tried to catch our breath. We were both sweating profusely, and our bodies were shaking uncontrollably.

"I sure hope the other guys wait a while before they go to our house," Reggie said with a shaky voice.

Once we began to calm down and breath normally, Reggie said, "We'd better get started home."

We had just left the brush field and had walked less than a block on Finley Street, when we heard sirens in the distance. The sound seemed to be coming from the direction of the Harrington Labs.

"It's either the ambulances, and they came to pick up the bodies, or it's the cops checkin' out the damage and lookin' for clues...or maybe both," Reggie noted resignedly.

I gulped hard and said, "Reg, do you think it's a good time to be goin' home?"

"Well, we told the other guys we'd meet 'em at the house, and we need to pow-wow so we can figure out what to do next," Reggie replied.

"Maybe we oughta turn ourselves in," I suggested. "This is gettin' real scary."

"Are you crazy?" Reggie shouted angrily. "You wanna go to jail for life?"

His straight-forward logic and ever-present power of persuasion left me without a reply.

When we arrived at the corner of Finley and Kimmel, we could hear the sirens blaring even louder. There was not much doubt about the origin of the sound.

Reggie and I hesitated a moment to scan in all directions before running up the steps to the Gearing's front porch.

Hidden out of sight, behind the 3-foot wall that surrounded the porch, were the other four culprits.

"Get down!" Spike barked nervously. "The cops just drove by here a couple a minutes ago."

As we all huddled on the porch, Reggie whispered, "It ain't safe here. Let's go out back and hide in my dad's tool shed."

We slipped off the porch and headed to the old wooden structure that sat in the northeast corner of the Gearing property. The tool shed, which measured approximately 12 by 20 feet, was actually a converted chicken house. Dad Gearing had remodeled the building for storage of tools and other seldom-used items that were taking up too much space in the house.

Two summers before, Dad Gearing had built four wooden bunk beds along one interior wall of the shed, so Reggie and I and some of our friends would have a place to 'sleep out' in the summer time. Since we no longer used the bunk beds for sleeping purposes, Dad had started using them as storage shelves for paint supplies and other things.

Reggie and I still maintained one corner of the shed for our club house. We had furnished the club house area with an old table, four wooden chairs, some orange crates, and an old kitchen cupboard, in which we hid some of our more private things.

We were all in the shed and seated around the table, when Spike said nervously, "Boy, I hope no one saw us come here. By the way, Reg, where's your Mom and the other kids?"

"Naw, I don't think anyone saw us," Reggie replied. "As for Mom, she went to visit my Aunt Helen — that's my Mom's older sister — and she took Luke and Briggete with her. Dad's gonna pick 'em up on his way home from the dairy."

We all watched as Reggie got up and walked over to the old kitchen cupboard. After opening one of the upper doors, he reached inside and pulled out a 3-pound coffee can.

"Would any of you guys like a smoke?" he asked, as he removed an almost full pack of cigarettes and a pack of matches from the can.

"Sure I'll take one," Spike responded.

"Me, too, Reg," I said eagerly.

"Count me in," Wally added.

"I'll pass. I got sick on 'em once," Dan said apologetically.

"I can't afford to have my ol' man smell cigarette smoke on me," Pete said sheepishly.

Reggie passed out cigarettes to the three of us and took one for himself. We were puffing away contentedly, when Spike, whose eyes were fixed intently on the shelves where the paint supplies were stored, asked, "Hey, Reg, what's in them brown, quart bottles...on the shelf under the paint cans?"

"Oh, that's some of Dad's home-brew beer," Reggie replied. "My Dad and my Uncle Ed whipped that batch up about a week ago. They bottle a new batch of home brew about every two or three months...whenever the supply's gettin' low. The new batch has to sit there and 'work' for awhile before it's ready to drink."

"Well, why does your dad keep the stuff out here, insteada' in the house?" Spike inquired.

"Cause, while it's workin', the bottles sometime explode. It's makes a helluva mess when that happens," Reggie explained.

"How long does it hafta work before it's ready for drinkin'?" Spike asked enthusiastically.

"Oh, about four or five days, accordin' to the temperature," Reggie replied authoritatively.

"Then this shit's ready right now, right, Reg?" Spike asked excitedly.

"Yeah, I guess so," Reggie answered, with a look of suspicion on his face. "What are you gettin' at, anyway?" Reggie demanded.

"Well, I was just thinkin'…Maybe we oughta sample us some of that home brew." Spike responded in a matter-of-fact manner.

"Are you shittin'? My dad would notice the missin' bottles right away." Reggie explained nervously.

"Not if he thought the bottles blew up," Spike argued. "We could leave a little beer in the bottles, and then break 'em and leave 'em on the shelf."

"Ya know, that just might work," Reggie conceded, "but no more than two bottles."

Reggie went to the storage shelves and removed two of the twenty bottles, and then walked over to the kitchen cupboard and sat the two quart bottles on the counter top. Standing in front of the cupboard, he reached down and pulled out the top utensil drawer, from which he removed a bottle opener.

When he popped off the first bottle cap, trapped carbon dioxide was released, causing a bluish vapor to curl up from the bottle.

"That shit sure looks potent," Spike said in wide-eyed amazement. Then, laughing nervously, he said, "Man, for a minute, I thought you released a genie or somethin'."

"My Dad says his home brew's got more than twice the alcohol content of store-bought beer," Reggie explained proudly.

"Well, who wants to go first?" Reggie asked, holding the bottle out in front of himself.

"Since it was my idea, I might as well be first," Spike replied eagerly. Reggie handed him the bottle.

Spike put the bottle to his lips and took a long draw of the brew. Having finished off several ounces of the liquid, he wiped his mouth with the back of his left hand, and handing the bottle to Reggie, said, "That ain't half bad. Reminds me of some of the church wine I snitched when I was servin' mass one time."

Reggie took a big swig from the bottle, and passed it to Wally, remarking, "Hell, it don't burn at all."

Not to be outdone, Wally held the bottle to his lips a long time. "Glug, glug, glug, glug," he went, until the contents were almost half gone.

"Take it easy, Wally. Save some for the rest of us," I said angrily, as I forcibly jerked the bottle away from him.

"I was just thirsty," Wally whined. "Hell, I ain't had nothin' to drink since early this mornin', and it's almost two-thirty now."

"Well, this shit can knock you on your ass," Reggie railed. "So just ease up, okay?"

"Don't worry about me, Reg, I can hold my booze," Wally said confidently.

I chugged down a fair quantity of the beer and handed the bottle to Dan. I had to agree with Spike, the home brew did taste a little like wine. Over the years, my Uncle Charlie had let Reggie and I sample small quantities of his homemade wines, unbeknownst to our parents.

Dan took a couple of swallows, and, handing the bottle to Pete, said, "This stuff is pretty good. Reminds me of hard-apple cider."

Pete was very hesitant to experiment with the rest of us. He probably felt he had the most to lose, because his dad was a policeman.

After considerable chiding from the rest of us, Pete relented and took a couple small sips. "I only hope my Dad doesn't smell this on my breath," he fretted, as he handed the bottle back to Spike.

Spike and Reggie each helped themselves to another healthy ration of the brew.

When Reggie had finished his second round, he said, "We'd better leave this little bit in the bottom of the bottle for breakin' later."

Reggie sat the first bottle back on the storage shelf, and then took a new bottle over to the cupboard and removed the cap. He handed the bottle to Wally, saying, "I believe it's your turn again, Wally. Try not to make a hog of yourself this time."

Wally downed a pretty good quantity of the beer, but not as much as the first. "Um-m-m," he said, as he passed the bottle to me.

I took another drink, and then Dan had his second.

Pete passed on the second round, saying he didn't want to push his luck.

My face was beginning to feel warm, and a numbness was forming around my mouth. Feeling a little self-conscious, I glanced over at Wally to see if he was looking at me. He was just standing there with a silly grin on his face.

Spike and Reggie finished their third ration of the home brew, leaving the bottle with about one-quarter of its original contents.

Wally tipped the bottle up, and, leaning his head back to receive the tempting drink, staggered backwards and would have fallen, had it not been for the wall in back of him. He somehow managed a couple of big gulps before handing me the bottle.

After finishing my third drink and handing the bottle to Dan, I began having problems focusing my eyes…My head was spinning, and everything in my line of vision was getting fuzzy.

Dan finished off all but a small quantity of the beer. He staggered forward as he handed the bottle to Reggie.

By this time, Wally was leaning against the cupboard for support, and Spike was sitting on a chair at the table, with his head down and cradled in his folded arms.

Pete was just standing by door, smiling and taking in the whole scene.

"I better take theesh' bottles over to the shelves and break 'em," Reggie said, noticeably slurring his words as he spoke.

Reggie stumbled over to the storage shelves, grabbing the backs of the chairs along the way for support. He rearranged the full bottles left on the shelves, opening up a small area in the center of the cluster. He then placed the two depleted bottles, one in each hand, over the empty area and swung them together sharply. The broken glass and residual liquid were deposited fairly evenly on the surface of the shelf. I thought the results looked pretty realistic — as if the bottles had really blown up their own.

Reggie stood with his back to the wooden shelves and, looking around the room at the rest of us, said, "We'd better get the hell outta here before my dad gets home. Let's sneak down to the Labs and see how much damage was done. It's been about an hour and a half since we heard the crash. The workers should be gone home for the night, and all the cops shoulda' cleared out by now."

I shaded my eyes with my hands as I stumbled out of the tool shed and into the bright sunshine.

As we walked slowly in the direction of the Harrington Labs, it was obvious that the effects of the alcohol had left everyone with varying degrees of unsteadiness—with the exception of Pete, who had consumed the least amount of anyone. Most of us staggered along the way, and a couple of the guys actually stumbled and fell, and had to be helped to their feet. We must of have looked like a parade of off-balance zombies to anyone who chanced to observe us in our inebriated condition.

We waited in the natural concealment of the small wooded area behind the Campfield Street houses, where we peered down the hill to recon' the Labs' property. From our vantage point, we could scan almost the entire landscape from east to west. It appeared that all activity around the Labs' complex had ceased.

Without a word, Reggie lifted his right arm vertically and then thrust it forward, signaling the rest of us to follow his lead.

As we neared the bottom of the hill, behind the Labs' main building, the aftermath of the runaway boxcar began to materialize. A few gasps were evident, as we stood wide-eyed with gaping mouths, digesting the full extent of the devastation. At that moment, my heart started pounding hard in my chest, and I felt an urge to start running again.

The catastrophic scene before us provided ample proof of the destructive force of a free-moving boxcar.

The ten-foot chain-link gate at the entrance of the Labs' loading-unloading compound had been blasted open with such force that both gates were nothing but masses of twisted metal — still hanging on their hinges, but laid back against the inside of the adjoining fence. Farther inside the compound were 60-gallon metal drums that had been ripped apart and strewn about by the impact, and whose liquid contents formed greenish puddles along both sides of the railroad track.

The forward momentum of the boxcar had finally been halted by the thick concrete structure that formed the foundation of the raised loading dock. Unfortunately, the front of the boxcar had carved a three-foot deep, four-foot long, V-shaped piece of concrete out of the loading dock.

The awesome scene of destruction seemed, very much in the literal sense, to have a sobering effect on us. I, for one, didn't feel the effects of the alcohol nearly as much as I had before.

Pete broke the silence, exclaiming, "We're all gonna go to jail for this, and my dad will probably be thrown off the police force!"

Reggie, in an attempt to calm Pete, said, "The damage can be fixed, and probably nobody got hurt. At least, I don't remember seein' any guys workin' out here when the boxcar broke loose."

"Now that you mention it, Reg, I don't recall anybody workin' outside either," Spike added reassuringly. "And besides, I don't see no blood or body parts anywhere."

"Thanks a helluva lot, Spike. That really helps," Pete said derisively.

"We better not stand here any longer, or somebody will see us for sure. Let's go back in the College Woods and figure out what to do next," Reggie said with a sense of urgency.

I glanced at my watch as we headed toward the woods. It was 4:15.

In less than 5 minutes, we arrived at a clearing near the swampy area. The clearing was surrounded by thickets and offered ideal concealment.

We stood there looking at each other, everyone wearing a worried expression, when Reggie inquired, "Well, any suggestions?"

"Maybe we oughta turn ourselves in and "face the music," Dan volunteered.

"To hell with that noise. I can't take that chance," Pete said adamantly. "I say we all take an oath of secrecy and just ride it out. If they question us, we'll hafta have a lie ready — like we were somewhere in the College Woods at the time."

"Well, I think we oughta hop a freight to Chicago and stay there until the whole thing blows over," Spike proposed. "We could all stay a couple days with my brother John."

"Well, we got three suggestions. I guess we'll hafta take a vote," Reggie said. "All in favor of Spike's idea — to run away to Chicago — raise their hands." Only Spike raised his hand.

"Okay, who's in favor of Dan's idea — to turn ourselves in?" Reggie asked.

Both Dan and Wally raised their hands. But when Wally looked around and saw that no one else favored the idea, he dropped his hand sheepishly, leaving Dan as the only assenter.

"Let's see a show of hands for Pete's plan — to cook up a story about being somewhere else at the time of the boxcar accident," Reggie ordered.

Reggie, Pete, Wally, and I raised our hands.

"That does it. Pete's idea wins." Reggie proclaimed.

"Now we'll need a damn good cover story…one that everybody will have to swear to if they get grilled," Pete pronounced.

"How about this? We were back at the Clay Banks playin' when it happened." I suggested.

"That's a good idea, Mark," Reggie said flatteringly. "In fact, we oughta run back there now and get our feet covered with that gooey clay before we head home."

"Great idea, Reg," Pete chimed in. "Let's get goin'. I hafta be home by five."

"Just remember, guys, nobody knows nothin' about that boxcar," Reggie warned. "Everybody raise their hand and swear to say that we were back at the Clay Banks most of the afternoon?" he demanded.

We all raised our hands and swore to tell the same story if asked our whereabouts at the time of the boxcar crash.

Reggie headed out first, on a dead run toward the Clay Banks. The rest of us followed.

The Clay Banks rose up steeply from the creek. From the main path that marked the top of the embankment, it was probably 80 feet to the water below. The steep bank on the other side of the creek was topped by the Erie railroad tracks. The Clay Banks were so named because the steep embankment was covered by a gray, viscid substance that ran 3 to 4 feet deep. Ordinary body weight could cause a person to sink waist-deep in the quagmire. Pulling oneself free took extreme effort and usually resulted in the loss of one or both shoes.

We stood on the main path looking down on the Clay Banks, when Reggie asked, "Okay, who's gonna be first to get their feet wet?" He hesitated, and then said laughingly, "Make that *muddy*."

"I guess I can be first," I said. "How deep do ya think I oughta go in, Reg?"

"Hell, just go in ankle deep," Reggie replied. "All you gotta do is sit on the edge of the bank and push your feet down in the clay. If ya stand up in the damn stuff, we'll probably hafta pull ya out."

Adhering to Reggie's suggestion, I sat on the very edge of the bank and pushed both my feet down hard into the sticky, gray substance. I stopped pushing once my feet were immersed almost to the top of my "clod-hoppers," nearly three inches above my ankles.

With great difficulty, I pulled my feet free from the glue-like substance that held them captive. The sucking action of my shoes breaking free from the clay created a strange slurping sound.

The clay, however, had done its job. A thick layer of the grayish goo clung tightly to both of my shoes, leaving no doubt that I had spent some time at the infamous Clay Banks. So much clay had collected on the bottoms of my shoes, that I had a difficult time standing upright without rocking from side to side. All I could think of at the time, though, was how much hard work It would take for me to return my shoes to their original condition.

Having observed how successful I had been in applying the clay to my shoes, the other guys began seating themselves on the edge of the bank in order to perform the same procedure.

I don't know what possessed Spike to do what he did, but as Wally was squatting to take his seat at the edge of the Clay Banks, Spike rushed up behind him and gave him a mighty shove. Wally was launched into space — looking as if he were taking flight, with his arms outstretched in front of him — and belly-smacked "Kersplat" in the glutinous substance, some 10 feet below us.

As he lay on his stomach, halfway buried in the thick ooze, Wally screamed in a stuttering fashion, "y-y-y-you, s-s-s-son of a b-b-bitch, I'm gonna kill ya, if I ever g-g-get outta here!" "C'mon, somebody help me, before I sink deeper!" he cried out hysterically.

Reggie shot a fierce look at Spike, and yelled angrily, "Why the hell did you hafta do that?"

"Well, I just thought it would look more realistic if one guy was really messed up," Spike explained apologetically.

"So you volunteered Wally for the job, huh?" Reggie barked. "Boy, that was a dumb-ass thing to do. Well, now we're gonna hafta get him out somehow."

"Don't move, Wally!" Reggie shouted. "We'll get a tree limb so we can pull ya outta there."

Within an instant, Dan came dragging a good sized limb to the edge of the bank. "Ya think this'll do the job, Reg?" he asked.

"Yeah, it's sure long enough." Reggie replied. "I just hope it's strong enough. It looks like it's been on the ground for a long while."

Reggie, Dan, and I each grabbed hold of the big limb and began sliding the small end forward, a little at a time. We finally had the smaller half of the big limb poised over Wally' back, with the very tip dangling a couple of inches above and in front of his hands.

"Nice and easy, Wally," Reggie cautioned. "We don't wanna break it, if we don't hafta."

Wally reached up, and as he made contact with his right hand, he called out, "Push it forward some, fellas, so I can get hold of a thicker part."

We were able to push the limb forward for another two feet, before Reggie, who was manning the last position on the large end, yelled, "That's enough, guys! Anymore, and I won't have nothin' ta hold on to."

Wally, who was facing downhill, managed to grab the limb firmly with both hands. We would somehow have to pull him around so his head would be pointing in our direction.

The three of us holding onto the large end of the limb took a couple of steps to the left and then began pulling hard. Wally, whose arms were stretched out taut in front of him, began to rotate slowly in our direction. Seemingly excited by the sudden progress, Pete and Spike, who had been just standing idly by, jumped in and each grabbed a piece of the big limb. The effect of the extra pulling power was immediately obvious. Wally's body, which had been half-buried in the clay, had been raised several inches and was now floating on the surface. Our latest effort had also rotated Wally a few more feet in our direction. Assuming Wally had started out pointing at 12 o'clock on an imaginary clock, we had managed to pull him around to about the 9 o'clock position.

The more we rotated him to the direction facing us, the greater gripping area we gained on the limb.

All of sudden, Wally screamed, "Hold up, fellas! I need to rest my arms for a minute. You nearly jerked 'em outta the socket the last time."

The five of us at the top of the Clay Banks squatted down and loosened our hold on the limb, taking advantage of the short rest period. Wally rested as best he could, while hanging onto the limb with just his right hand.

After two or three minutes, Reggie terminated the brief respite by standing up and shouting, "We'd better get with it, fellas! It's gettin' pretty late!"

My watch was showing 5:05, as we at the top took our positions on the large end of the limb. Wally again grabbed the smaller end with both hands.

Our new effort paid dividends quickly. Wally was immediately rotated completely around; his head was now pointed in our direction. He pulled his head up as far as possible and arched his neck backward in order to peer up the incline to where the rest of us were collected.

He looked anything but human as we continued to pull him up the incline. Wally was almost completely covered with a heavy layer of the sticky, gray goo. There were only a couple clear areas on his entire body; the raised part of his buttocks, and a small area between his shoulder blades. His earlier thrashing about had left his head completely encased in the substance. Only his eyeballs and teeth showed through the clay mask. It took a superhuman effort by everyone just to keep from laughing at his bizarre appearance.

We had finally pulled him to the top of the bank. Reggie reached out and grabbed Wally's hands, pulling him onto the path where the rest of us stood.

Wally stood up with great difficulty. The weight of the clay probably added another 50 pounds to his body.

As Wally stood there looking so pitiful, Spike, who could hold back no longer, burst into raucous laughter. The rest of us joined in, laughing hysterically until tears rolled down our cheeks.

Wally just stood there glaring at us. His fiery, brown eyes, peering out from under his clay-laden eyelids, clearly showing his intense anger

Spike, still cackling with laughter, pointed at Wally and said, "Do you know who he looks like?" "Hell, he's the spittin' image of the *Mummy*." "Drag your right foot when you walk, Wally," he taunted.

Wally had had enough. He could take no more. Like a bolt of lighting he leaped at Spike, knocking him to the ground. Once he was on top of Spike, Wally grabbed him tightly and the two rolled over and over in the dusty pathway. It became readily apparent that Wally was not trying to hurt Spike; he was merely trying to share some of his surplus clay with him. The furious body contact and rubbing that Wally applied to Spike during their brief tussle did its job to perfection. Spike's body now shared a similar appearance to Wally's. Although Wally still wore the bulk of the gray ooze, Spike was fairly well covered with a combination of gray clay and dust.

As soon as Wally released his hold, Spike jumped to feet, blustering, "You son-of-a-bitch!" "Why did you hafta go and do somethin' like that?"

Wally, smiling through clay-encased lips, replied mockingly, "Well, I just thought it'd look even more realistic if two of us got really messed up."

The rest of us convulsed in laughter. The "devil" had finally gotten his dues.

Everyone remained unusually quiet as we walked out of the College Woods. I guess we were all worried about the consequences of the incident at the Harrington Labs. I know I had visions of the cops greeting Reg and I when we arrived home.

By he time we reached the north end of Finley Street, Spike and Wally were looking pretty pathetic and were having a difficult time keeping up with rest of us. The clay covering the exposed parts of their bodies and their clothing had dried and hardened to a cement-like consistency; the light-gray, powdery coating giving them a ghostly appearance. Their trousers and shirts had become board-like — in much the same way that clothing gets when overly starched. The rest of us had difficulty in suppressing our laughter.

We had progressed about a block down Finley Street, when Luke came running up from the Gearing house to meet us. As he approached us, he yelled breathlessly, "Hey, where you guys been?"

"We been playin' out at the Clay Banks. Can't ya tell?" Reggie replied cautiously. "What's goin' on anyway?"

"Well, all I can say is, you missed somethin' really big," Luke replied excitedly. "There's been a big accident down at the Harrington Labs. Everybody in the neighborhood's talkin' about it."

"What kinda accident ya talkin' about?" Reggie probed.

"Well, the big boxcar that was parked on the spur line broke loose, rolled down the hill, and crashed into the side of the main building," Luke explained.

"Do they know how it happened?" Pete asked nervously.

Literally beaming to have all this attention from the big guys, Luke replied, "From what I hear, they figure that the brake just came loose and away she went."

"Well, was anybody hurt?" I finally asked.

"Naw. Heck, all the guys were inside at the time," Luke lamented. "Man, ya oughta see the damage, though. If you guys are interested, I'll show ya after supper. Okay?"

"I don't think so, Luke," Reggie replied. "We've had a pretty busy day ourselves. Huh, fellas?"

Pete, who was visibly showing his relief with a broad smile, said, "Yeah, I'd better head home, too. I'm pretty tired from all the activity today."

"I gotta get home and get this damn clay off me," Spike remarked. "Me, too," Wally added.

"I gotta go somewhere with my parents tonight," Dan explained.

"Well, does anybody feel like doin' somethin' tonight?" Spike asked.

We all declined the offer. I guess the rest of us felt pretty lucky that our day didn't end up a total disaster. We weren't about to "tempt the gods" any further.

Reggie and I, once inside the back porch, used a laundry brush and the water tap, which was located directly over the deep cone-shaped drain, to clean the clay from our shoes. We left our shoes on the back porch to dry and entered the kitchen.

Mom was standing at the stove, putting the finishing touches on our evening meal. Luke and Briggete were in the process of setting the supper table. Hearing the back-porch door close behind her, Mom turned around to face us. "Well, it's about time you boys got home," she scolded. "You know you're a half an hour late? We were beginning to worry about you; what with all the goings on around this neighborhood this afternoon."

"Geez, Mom, we're really sorry," Reggie said, showing as much remorse as he could muster. "Ya see, Wally fell into the mucky stuff at the Clay Banks, and we had to fish him out. By the way, how's Aunt Helen doin'?" he asked, trying to change the subject.

"She's doing fine," Mom replied. "Well, you'd better go into the front room now," she said somberly. And then she delivered the most dreaded words known to teenage boys: "Your dad's been waiting to talk to you."

Reggie and I walked slowly to the front room to "face the music." Dad, who had been sitting in his easy chair, reading the evening newspaper, glanced over his right shoulder and observed us sternly. "Were you boys in the tool shed this afternoon?" he demanded.

"Well, uh-uh-uh," Reggie stammered.

I had a large lump in my throat and couldn't say anything. *"He must have figured out about the beer,"* I thought to myself. *Oh, Lord, have mercy!"*

"Well, were you?" he barked.

After a long pause, Reggie, nodding his head slowly, volunteered, "Yeah, we were in there a little while." "Why, is somethin' wrong, Dad?" he asked nervously.

"You better damn well know there's somethin' wrong," Dad shouted angrily.

"Oh, Oh, here it comes," I thought to myself.

"I found a cigarette butt on the floor of the tool shed," Dad said, with a scowl on his face. "Can you boys explain that?" he demanded, turning to me and then to Reggie.

"Well, Dad," Reggie began to explain slowly, "Mark and me and some of the other guys did smoke that cigarette." "I know it was wrong and I'm sorry," he said, staring at the floor. I guess we just wanted to find out what it was like. "Besides, Dad, is that any worse than the chewin' tobacco you gave Mark and me that time on the milk route, and then laughed when we got sick?"

"You just keep quiet about that!" Dad said angrily. "I don't want your Mother to know about it. Anyway, I was just tryin' to teach you boys a lesson about the evils of tobacco."

"Now, what you boys did today was wrong and you know it," Dad explained in a calmer voice. "You coulda burned down the old shed. So for punishment you're gonna have to stay home tonight. And ya gotta promise me ya won't ever do anything like that again."

Reggie, who was great at the dramatics, rose to the occasion. "Geez, Dad," he said haltingly, as if on verge of tears, "We had some big plans for tonight." "Ya sure ya won't reconsider?" he pleaded, with his right hand covering his eyes, as if to catch the tears.

I caught the sideways wink that Reggie flashed at me from under his extended fingers — a very dangerous thing to do, considering what Dad might have done to us had he detected it.

"Well, do you boys promise never to do anything like that again?" Dad asked somberly. Reggie and I both said we were sorry and nothing like that would ever happen again.

"Well, I think you boys learned your lesson," Dad said, expressing his satisfaction. "So after supper, I want you to go directly to your bedroom. No radio or anything tonight, okay?"

We gladly agreed to the conditions.

At some point Dad's mood had transformed from one of extreme anger to one of pleasantness. "It'll be a few minutes until your Mom has supper ready," he noted. "Do you boys want to hear a good story?"

"Sure, Dad," Reggie replied eagerly. I nodded in agreement.

"Well, I finally got even with ol' Charlie Danowski today," he said proudly. "Remember, he screwed me on a gun deal a couple of months ago?"

"Ya mean the old polish guy who owns the Smoke House, down by the river?" I inquired. (The Smoke House was an establishment that combined a card parlor with a firearms business.)

"Yeah, that's him," Dad confirmed, his voice betraying his bitterness. "The son-of-a-bitch sold me a defective shotgun back in January. I took it out huntin' the day I bought it. When I kicked up my first rabbit and was lowering the barrel to draw a bead, both barrels went off in the air before I could even pull the trigger. Scared the hell outta me. I took it right back to Charlie, and he refused to refund my money. He said he was just gettin' even for all the times I had screwed him in gun deals in the past. I cussed him out good and told him he hadn't heard the last of it. I'd a kicked his ass, but I knew I'd be dealin' with him again.

It might be well at this time to explain Dad's love affair with gun-trading. It was not just his favorite hobby; it was an obsession with him. I think the uncontrollable urge to trade guns offered him the ultimate challenge of matching wits with the other guy. It may also have had something to do with his heritage. You see, his father, Charles Gearing, was an authentic, 19th-century pioneer, a man who survived in the wilderness by using his wits and the barter system.

My theory is that Dad was imbued with this same pioneer spirit, which not only gave him his love of guns, but also the desire to sell them for monetary gain or trade them to better his existing firearm collection. His collection was being turned over constantly. And even though he exhibited great fondness for some of his more rare guns, every one had its price.

A little background on Grandpa Gearing may be in order here. In 1871, as a young man of 21, Charles Gearing, with his new bride, traveled by covered wagon from Ohio to the Kansas Territory to seek his fortune. For several years, he made his living as a buffalo hunter. Later, when the buffalo population had been drastically depleted, he decided to homestead and try his hand at farming. He and his young family lived in a sod house and endured many hardships while trying to raise a successful corn crop. Finally, one year when their fortunes were beginning to look brighter, a plague of grasshoppers descended on their farm and wiped out their 50-acre corn crop, which was nearly ready for harvesting. Totally disheartened and virtually penniless, Grandpa and his family moved back to Ohio to start a new life.

After the death of his first wife in 1897, Grandpa went to Alaska to try his luck at prospecting for gold. This venture ultimately failed also, and he returned to Ohio. After being back home a short time, he began working for the Nickel Plate Railroad and married his second wife, my Grandmother. My father, Kenny, was next to the youngest of five children in Grandpa's second family.

So you see, my dad came from pretty sturdy stock and inbred in him, I think, were some of the pioneer characteristics that made the owning of guns and the act of trading them so important to him.

During the depression, Dad supplemented his paltry income from his dairy job with the proceeds gained from his private gun business. We could not have survived without this additional income.

During this period, pistols, rifles, and shotguns were stored throughout the Gearing house. It seemed that every dresser drawer and closet contained guns. I would estimate that his total cache of firearms, at times, numbered as many as two to three hundred. So guns around our house were always a natural part of our lives.

Dad explained that it took him a couple of weeks to cool down after his encounter with Charlie Danowski. So finally feeling a little better about their relationship, he decided to resume doing business with Charlie.

Dad related that he had a Westernfield lever-action, 12-gauge shotgun that he wanted to "unload" for cash. The gun, although very rare, was considered by gun experts to be a 'white elephant,' because of its shoddy workmanship.

One day after work, Dad took the gun to the Smoke House to see if he could interest Charlie in it. Unfortunately, Charlie was still chaffing from the cursing he had received during their last meeting, and he proceeded to treat Dad with extreme rudeness. He called Dad's merchandise a "piece of shit" and said he wouldn't display it next to his good guns even if he got it for nothing. One word led to another and Dad stormed out in a huff, with one thought in mind: to get even with Charlie Danowski.

It took Dad a couple of days to formulate his plan. On Good Friday, immediately after returning home from work, he cautiously covered the telephone receiver with a handkerchief and dialed up the Smoke House number. Charlie answered the phone and asked to whom was he speaking. Dad, disguising his voice as best he could and using a fictitious name, introduced himself as a traveling salesman who had found Charlie's establishment listed in the yellow pages. He said he was calling from a truck stop located on U.S. 24, east of Harrington.

"What can I do for you?" Charlie asked enthusiastically.

"Well, there's a certain 12-gauge, shotgun that I've been searching for all over the tri-state area," Dad explained. "It's made by Westernfield and it's a lever-action. I need it to complete my collection of rare shotguns. I'd be willing to pay a premium price for that particular gun. I don't suppose you've ever heard of one, have you?" During the long pause that followed, Dad said he could visualize Charlie salivating at the other end of the phone.

Charlie finally replied, "This must be your lucky day, Mister. I think I know where I might be able to pick up a gun like that, but it'll cost a lot to get it. When will you be coming through Harrington again?"

"I'll be back here in two weeks," Dad replied. "And remember, money's no object."

"I'll see you in two weeks," Charlie said, bubbling over with friendliness.

"Okay, I'll be looking forward to it," Dad said, as he hung up the phone.

"It wasn't more than a minute later, when the phone rang," Dad related. "Guess what? It was Charlie Danowski," he said, grinning from ear to ear. "Charlie said he called to apologize for our little misunderstanding, and to tell me that our business relationship was too important to him to lose. He said to prove his friendship, he would be willing to discuss a deal on that Westernfield shotgun that I had brought to his store."

Knowing he was close to "setting the hook," Dad replied, "Well, I don't know, Charlie. I've already got two solid offers on the gun. I could be passing up some big money."

In a very nervous voice, Charlie responded, "Look, Kenny, you bring the gun down here, and I'll beat the hell out of the other guys' offers. Your friendship means that much to me. Okay?"

After keeping Charlie waiting an adequate period of time, Dad finally said, "Well I guess so, Charlie. But you'll have to wait until Monday afternoon. That's the soonest I can get in to see you."

"Okay, I'll see you Monday, and you won't be sorry," Charlie said gratefully.

Dad had played ol' Charlie like a violin.

Dad continued his story with a description of how his appointment went with Charlie.

"Ol' Charlie almost shook my arm off when I showed up at the Smoke House this afternoon," Dad said, chuckling. "You woulda thought I was his long-lost brother."

Charlie gushed all over himself, saying, "Hi, Kenny, how's it going." "Gee, it's good to see you again. I see you brought the gun. Can I take a look at It?"

"Sure thing," Dad replied, as he handed the gun over the counter to Charlie.

As Charlie was moving the gun around under the light, inspecting it from all angles, he asked, "What do ya hafta have for this old gun, Ken?"

After an appropriate pause, Dad replied slowly, "Well, to tell the truth, Charlie, I've got about $125 tied up in the gun. I don't think I could take less than $150. Ya know, we gun dealers hafta realize a little profit." (Dad had actually invested $50 in the gun, and top-book on the weapon was about $75.)

Charlie seemed to choke for a moment at Dad's asking price. Coughing as if to clear his throat, he finally said, "You know as well as I do, Kenny, that the gun ain't worth that much. Now, what's your absolute bottom dollar, ol' buddy?"

"Well, for you, Charlie, I guess I'd be willin' to give up most of my normal profit," Dad said, feigning a pained expression. "Mind you, I wouldn't do this for anyone else. So, how about $130 for my gun, and you throw in a couple boxes of 12-gauge, 6-shot ammo, just to sweeten the deal a bit?"

"That's a deal, ol' buddy," Charlie responded, literally beaming.

As Dad was leaving the establishment, Charlie, who was grinning like the Cheshire Cat, slapped Dad on the back, saying, "See you soon, ol' buddy."

Dad, feeling very good about himself, also, bid Charlie farewell, and left the store, whistling. He told us that he planned never to do business with Charlie again, but that he would give just about anything to see ol' Charlie's reaction when he finally realizes that his mystery buyer will never show up.

Reggie and I laughed heartily at the story and complimented Dad on the ingenious way he evened the score with Charlie.

Immediately after supper that night, in compliance with Dad's earlier order, Reggie and I went upstairs to the comfort of the big, old double bed that we shared. We talked a long time before finally falling asleep. We reviewed the day's events in detail and agreed that we'd been really lucky not to have been in a lot more trouble. Considering the circumstances, going to bed early seemed a small price to pay.

'Playing' with Dynamite

Tuesday morning looked like the beginning of another beautiful spring day. Reggie and I, anxious to start the new day, were out of bed by 8:30. Before falling asleep the night before, we had discussed how much fun it would be to ride our bikes out to the old Lime Quarry, for another day of big adventure.

When we arrived downstairs, we were greeted with a delicious aroma emanating from the kitchen. Mom was in the process of frying a sizeable quantity of bacon and eggs, and as a special treat, she was deep-frying some of her "world-famous" doughnuts, which, after removing them from the hot grease, she sprinkled liberally with sugar and cinnamon.

Reggie and I bid Mom a good morning, and then stopped at the stove for a moment to check out our breakfast in progress and inhale the tantalizing smells up close.

"U-m-m-m, smells real good, Mom," Reggie commented appreciatively.

Mom smiled, and said, "You boys get washed up now. Breakfast will be ready in about five minutes."

After returning from the bathroom, Reggie and I sat down at the table. Mom had just begun serving up the meal, when I looked up at her and asked, "Aren't Luke and Briggete gonna be eatin' with us?"

"Oh my, no," she replied. "They both ate earlier. Luke is already outside playing with a friend, and Briggete is out in the side yard, playing in her sandbox."

As we began "digging in," Reggie asked, "Mom, do we have any chores to do today?"

"Only the dishes, after you've finished your breakfast." she answered.

"Sounds great, Mom," Reggie responded, with a big smile. "That means we got all day to do what we want." Mom nodded her agreement.

"By the way," continued Reggie, "Would it be possible for me and Mark to take a packed lunch with us today? Ya see, we'd like to get some of the other guys and ride our bikes out to the Lime Quarry."

Mom, concern showing on her face, replied sternly, "Well, I don't mind you boys being gone all day, but that old quarry is a very dangerous place, what with all that deep water and the blasting that's going on at that new quarry, nearby. I don't know how I'd ever explain it to your father if something were to happen to you boys, and it was my fault."

"You don't hafta worry about us, Mom," I pleaded. "We've been out there a lotta times and never got hurt."

"It's too darn cold to go swimmin', anyway," Reggie chimed in. "How 'bout if we promise to stay away from the new quarry while their usin' dynamite?"

"Well, I guess it'll be okay," she finally relented. "But I'll be worried until you get home this afternoon. Go ahead and call your friends now, while I pack your lunches. You can carry your sack lunches in that old canvas newspaper bag, hanging on the back porch."

"Gee, thanks, Mom. You're "one in a million," Reggie said gratefully. "And I promise we'll be real careful."

Reggie called the other guys, and all but Dan could go with us. Dan's brother Bernie had just gotten home on leave from the Navy.

The plan was that we would all meet at Pete's house at 10:00 o'clock.

The old lime quarry was about 3 miles east of where we lived. It was located less than one-quarter mile south of Highway 24. All in all, it was about a 10-minute ride by bicycle.

The quarry, which was oval-shaped and covered about 15 acres, was said to have been "worked-out" a long time before. Apparently, after all the accessible limestone had been removed, it was abandoned and left to fill up with water. The water in the deepest part of the quarry was estimated to be 65 to 80 feet deep. Underground springs replenished the water supply constantly, leaving the water always cool and clear.

The sheer, vertical walls of the quarry were formed by layered, flat rocks and, for the most part, rose to about 20 feet above the water. In one place, there was a natural step formation in the rock that led down to a huge flat rock that jutted 10 feet out into the water. It was on this big rock that we congregated to swim and fish.

About 100 feet from the south-west corner of the quarry laid the remains of an old lime kiln. The 150-foot long structure that housed the eight brick-lined ovens, when viewed from a distance, resembled one wall of an old fortress with eight entrances near its base. The entire brick structure was built on a 20-foot mound of earth. The ovens themselves were dome-shaped, and appeared as inverted u-shaped openings in the face of the 30-foot high stone wall.

The ovens were approximately six feet high at the peak of the domed ceiling and eight feet wide. They were lined with fire brick, and the dome-shaped tunnels ran entirely through the 15-foot thick wall, leaving the same size openings on both sides. The circular, 6-foot opening in the middle of the oven ceiling provided the opening to the chimney, which exited through the top of the wall. An 8-foot wide, stone walkway was provided along the north side of the ovens.

Earth that had been mounded up at the west end of the walled structure provided an inclined walkway from ground level to the top of the structure. This walkway was said to have been used as a pathway for the man-guided mules that conveyed the limestone slabs that were to be "fired" in the ovens below. The heating of the limestone was the first step in the process of extracting the lime.

Ultimately, the lime deposits from the stones were pulverized into the fine, powdery substance that most people recognize as lime.

As history tells it, the lime-kiln structure was built in the 1880s and used for 30 to 40 years before a large explosion and fire caused the operation to be terminated and the facility to be abandoned. The explosion and resulting fire was said to have taken several human lives, in addition to destroying a number of the work mules. Bricks from the outer walls and from the kiln ovens lay in heaps outside the structure.

The old, abandoned lime-kiln, in addition to other nearby land-marks, offered many excellent hiding places for our impromptu games of "slips." A rickety, old water tower stood near the lime-kiln works. About 100 feet south of the lime-kiln structure, with the Wabash Railroad tracks running along its south side, was what we called the old "Lime Building." We arrived at the name, because there was ample evidence that the 200-foot long building had been used to process and package lime. Lime residue was spread in profusion throughout the building. You couldn't walk through the interior without picking up the powdery white substance on your shoes and clothing.

Usually, when we exited the building, we'd be so covered with the powdery white dust that we would've taken on the appearance of ghosts. The only good way to remove our chalky white armor was with a dip in the quarry, clothes and all.

One quarter-mile west of the old lime-quarry complex was a new, active limestone quarry, where limestone was being mined every day. The new quarry, which was probably three times the size of the old one and over 100 feet deep, was being constantly pumped free of the spring water that flowed into it. A large, ramped driveway on its west end led down into the quarry. The bottom of the quarry was checkered with a network of roads, which the big dump trucks used to haul out the slabs of limestone. Dynamite blasting, used to cleave out huge walls of lime-stone, was an on-going process.

One of our most favorite things was to lie along the quarry's rim, concealed like spies in the deep grass, and monitor the whole quarry operation. We always made sure that we were on the side opposite where the blasting was being conducted. It was thrilling to hear the warning whistle, and then witness the big charges being fired off. The charges were 20-inch sticks of dynamite that were placed into vertical holes that had been drilled in the quarry's rim, approximately 15 feet from the edge.

When the big charges were set off, a tremendous roar would be heard, and the ground would tremble as if an earthquake were occurring. A big wall of limestone would then break away and rumble down to the quarry floor. In what seemed to be a slow-motion depiction, great clouds of dust would roll up into the sky and then settle slowly back into the quarry. We were always awed by the spectacle.

As soon as the dust cleared at the bottom of the quarry, the big cranes would go to work picking up the huge limestone slabs and filling up the waiting dump trucks.

Just as planned, everyone showed up at Pete's by 10:00 o'clock. The bicycle ride along highway 24 was uneventful until we were about one-half mile from the quarry. Suddenly, Spike, sporting a devilish grin, began to speed up, leaving the rest of us in his wake. By the time he was about 30 yards in front of us and picking speed, the rest of us got the message and took up the challenge. It wasn't long until Reggie, pedaling like a demon, was only about 20 feet behind Spike, and gaining fast. Pete, Wally, and I were strung out behind them. Wally, trailing me by 50 feet or so, was bringing up the rear. We were all giving it our best effort as Reggie arrived first at the turnoff road to the quarry, with Spike right on his tail. Only one-quarter of a mile to the quarry.

It was amazing how fast Reggie could go, especially since that old canvas bag stretched across his handlebars had to create a substantial amount of wind resistance.

Reggie was now leading Spike by at least 100 feet, as we raced down the gravel road that ran past the entrance to the old Lime Quarry property. Pete and I had gained ground and were now right behind Spike, who was beginning to tire, and the angry look on his face was strong evidence of his growing frustration. Poor old Wally had fallen even farther behind, and was now trailing the three of us by some 50 yards.

Spike, Pete, and I were literally eating Reggie's dust on that dried-out, old gravel road. It was becoming increasingly difficult to discern Reggie's form through the cloud of dust he had created. We three, who were closely bunched far behind him, were sweating profusely, causing the dust particles to cling like glue to our exposed arms and faces.

As we strained mightily to gain ground on Reggie, we could faintly hear, from far behind, Wally's plaintive appeal: "Wait up, fellas. I got a charlie horse in my right leg, and it's hurtin' real bad."

Spike looked back over his shoulder at Pete and me, smirking, and said sarcastically, "Now, ain't that just too bad about poor ol' Wally?"

All out of breath and covered with dust, Spike, Pete, and I skidded to a stop almost simultaneously at the base of lime-kiln structure. Reggie, who was sitting nonchalantly on a pile of bricks next to his bike, as if he had been there for a long time, was grinning smugly. "What took you guys so long?" he asked.

"I'd a caught your ass, Reg, if you hadn't throwed so damn much dust back at us," Spike retorted. "I was afraid to get too close. I coulda caught a stone in the eye."

"Yeah, yeah, we know." Reggie replied mockingly. "Anyway, you'll get a chance to prove how fast you are on the way back." "Now, where the hell is Wally?" he asked impatiently.

"There he is, just comin' in the entrance, pushin' his bike," I replied.

Wally, limping and ashen-faced, was making moaning sounds as he reached the spot where the rest of us sat on the brick pile. He glared at us momentarily and then threw his bike down hard and dropped to the ground. Holding his right side, he yelled, "I coulda killed myself back there and you guys wouldn't a give a damn! O-h-h-h-h!"

"You pathetic shit. What's wrong with you now?" Spike said contemptuously.

"Oh nothin' at all," Wally shot back sarcastically. "The chain slipped on my old bike and I busted my balls real bad on the crossbar. I'll probably never be able to have any kids now," he blubbered.

"No big deal," Spike replied, smirking at the rest of us. "You'd never be able to find a woman in the first place. Huh, fellas?"

We all laughed uproariously, and Wally turned away to suffer in silence.

After a minute or so, Reggie walked over to Wally and put his hand on his shoulder. "How ya doin', Wally?" he said caringly. "Feel like playin' some slips now?"

"Yeah, I guess so," Wally said haltingly. "But I don't wanna be "It" first. I'm still hurtin'."

"Hell, I'll be "It" first," Spike volunteered. "I'll count to a hundred, and then I'll come lookin'."

The four of us who were to be hunted by Spike headed off in different directions, looking for the perfect hiding place.

The next few hours were spent playing slips. We all had our turns at being "It" and scouring the entire compound in search of the hiders. It was great fun, but the mid-day sun began to take its toll.

It was about 2:30 in the afternoon when we sat down at the base of the old water tower to rest and eat our packed lunches. While we ate voraciously, we discussed the best hiding places of the day. If someone had found an exceptionally good hiding place, one where they were never detected and were allowed to come home "free", the rest of us would work hard on that individual to wheedle out his secret location. Hardly ever would anyone divulge his hiding place, because it could always be used the next time.

As we sat talking, the 3:00 o'clock stop-work whistle at the new quarry sounded.

Reggie held up his right hand to quiet the rest of us. "Hear that. The guys at the new quarry are gonna be goin' home now. Let's wait a few minutes and then go over and check it out. We've never been down inside the quarry before. There's a lot of machinery and neat things down there."

"Sounds like fun to me," I said enthusiastically.

"Yeah, but you better not get caught down there," Pete warned. "There's "No Trespassing" signs all over the place."

"Aw, let's give it a shot," Spike said matter-of-factly. "Ain't nobody gonna catch us."

We all rose and started walking in the direction of the new quarry.

We walked around the south rim of the quarry until we arrived at the west end, where the ramped roadway ran down to the quarry floor.

As we started down the ramp, Reggie said, "Well, it looks pretty quiet down there. I'd say everybody's left by now."

"Yeah, but what if they got a night watchman?" Wally said nervously.

"Don't worry about a watchman," Pete said. "My dad said that the city police patrol this place once every hour, starting at 7:00 o'clock."

Once at the bottom, everyone spread out to investigate all the nooks and crannies of this exciting new world.

Some of the guys climbed on the big cranes or dump trucks to play around with the controls. As I followed Reggie down a dusty road toward the middle of the quarry, I saw Spike heading toward the pump house.

It was obvious that Reggie was heading to the area where the wooden shack and three large steel chests were located.

When I had caught up to Reggie, he was standing in front of one the rusty steel chests. The chest was about four-feet high, four-feet deep, and eight-feet long. Its 1/2-inch thick, hinged lid was secured with a huge padlock.

"Ya know what this looks like? " Reggie asked, trying hard to contain his excitement.

"I know it's somethin' they don't want ya to get into," I responded, my shaky voice betraying my uneasiness.

"Hell, this is probably where they keep their explosives," Reggie said, grinning broadly. "I'm gonna open this baby up and see what's inside."

I felt a sinking feeling coming over me — a dark feeling of foreboding.

I knew there was no chance of dissuading Reggie from carrying out his next action. He had already begun pounding on the big lock with a piece of lime stone.

Reggie worked furiously on the lock. He pounded so hard that chips of stone flew out in all directions. The sweat had beaded up on his forehead, when he stopped for a minute to rest his arm.

"You're not gonna open that up, Reg. Just give it up," I pleaded.

"Like hell I won't," Reggie barked determinedly, as he began crashing the heavy stone against the lock again.

All of a sudden, as if by magic, the big padlock sprung open with a clanging sound.

Perspiring heavily by this time, Reggie turned to me and shouted, "Help me lift the lid on this damn thing, will ya!"

It was all the two of us could do to lift the creaky steel lid and push it back on its hinges.

We both stood in amazement, looking down inside the big chest. There in front of us were hundreds of six-inch dynamite sticks. Each of the cylindrical, red sticks was covered with a waxy paper outer wrap, emblazoned in black letters with the label "60% Gelatin Dynamite."

"We gotta have some of these!" Reggie exclaimed, gleefully.

I felt a cold chill go up my spine.

"Hey, fellas, come see what we found," Reggie shouted excitedly, waving his arms in the air.

Spike was the first to arrive and peer inside the chest. "Holy shit, dynamite!" he sputtered. "We hit the mother lode, sure as hell!"

By this time, the rest of the guys, awestruck and with mouths agape, were also peering inside the big steel chest.

Pete was the first to speak, his nervousness apparent, "If you guys think you can do anything with this, you're fulla' shit! I happen to know that you gotta have fuses and blasting caps to make dynamite work. So you might as well forget the whole thing. Let's get the hell outta here."

Wally, with a wide-eyed expression, quickly added, "I'll second that!"

"Hell, everybody knows you gotta have fuses and caps to blow up dynamite," Reggie countered. "They gotta have 'em stashed around here someplace, and we're gonna find 'em."

"In fact, I think I know where they keep the fuses and caps," Reggie stated, looking back over his shoulder in the direction of a padlocked shed, located about one hundred feet to the rear of us.

Before anyone could speak, Reggie had run to the red-painted shed and was working over the padlock with another piece of lime stone. He seemed almost demon-like in his fervor to open the second lock.

As we all stood behind him, watching, the second lock gave way to Reggie's determination.

Reggie was right. The shelves inside the shed were virtually filled with bundles of 5- and 20-minute coiled fuses, each tipped with a shiny, copper-colored blasting cap. Four pieces of binding twine were used as ties along the circumference of each bundle to keep the coils together. There were 10 fuse-blasting cap combinations secured in each bundle.

"Man, we can have some big fun now!" Spike exclaimed, as he began grabbing for the fuses.

Reggie immediately grabbed Spike by the arm and spun him around, while blaring in his face, "You crazy shit! Do you want to get us all blowed up? You hit a couple of those fuse caps together and we all go up in smoke! Those things are filled with nitro!"

"Geez, I'm sorry, Reg," Spike replied apologetically. "I thought you had to light the damn things before they could blow up."

Turning around to face the rest of us, Reggie said in a much calmer voice, "Look, guys, If we're gonna take any of this stuff, we've gotta be more careful. From here on, I'll be givin' the orders."

Reggie walked back to the dynamite chest, reached in and pulled out two dynamite sticks. Holding the sticks in the air, he said, "I helped my Uncle Art do some blastin' on his farm last summer. So I think I'm the closest thing to an expert here."

Waving the two sticks in the air, Reggie continued his dissertation, as the rest of us listened with rapt attention from a safe distance away. "Actually, these dynamite sticks are pretty harmless by themselves," he stated in an authoritative manner. "See," he said, as he banged them together, causing the rest of us to jump back a few more feet. We stood there wide-eyed and shaken, anxiously awaiting the next words of wisdom from the "Master."

Smiling arrogantly, obviously pleased with himself, Reggie continued: "Ya see, what ya really have to be careful of is the blasting caps on the end of the fuses. Those little fellas hafta be handled real careful 'cause even by themselves, they can blow up worse than any firecracker you ever saw. Now, I don't need to demonstrate that fact, do I?"

"Hell no! We believe ya, Reg." Wally said nervously.

"Well then, the next step is that each one of us is gonna hafta carry a share of the explosives back to the bicycles," Reggie stated matter-of-factly.

I thought I heard a unified gulp.

"Anyway, to make it easy on you guys," Reggie continued, "I'll carry all the fuses, and you can carry the easy stuff. Okay?"

"Sounds fair to me," Spike responded gratefully.

"Okay, then, each of you guys take six sticks of dynamite," Reggie ordered. "I'll get six bundles of 5-minute fuses."

"Let's see, that'll make 24 sticks of dynamite and 30 fuses. It won't hurt ta have a few extra fuses," Reggie mused.

Reggie proceeded to gingerly pass out the dynamite to the rest of us. Spike and I stepped up readily to accept our "fair share." As expected, Pete and Wally were not as compliant They protested loudly as to how physically dangerous it was and how, if we're caught with explosives, we'd go to prison for a long time.

After absorbing considerable ridicule from Reggie, Spike, and me, Pete and Wally reluctantly accepted their quotas.

Once loaded up, the four "dynamite-pack mules" and Reggie, with both hands full of fuses, headed off to the lime-kiln structure, where our bikes were parked.

As we arrived back at the brick pile, Spike looked down at his bicycle and then shot an angry look at Reggie. "Reg, how the hell are we 'sposed to ride our bikes with our hands fulla dynamite?"

"Don't get your jockeys in a bind, Spike. I gotcha covered," Reggie said cockily. We're gonna put all the explosives in the old canvas bag I brought, and I'll even volunteer to carry everything on my bike. Hell, I just remembered, I got a couple of old issues of the Harrington Herald Press in the bag. I can use sheets of paper to wrap the fuse bundles separately. They'll be a lot safer that way. How about that? Am I a genius, or what?"

"Yeah, you're really somethin', Reg," I replied, winking at Spike. "Trouble is, they ain't found a name for it yet."

"Well, let's get this show on road," Reggie said, as he began taking our dynamite and carefully placing the sticks in the canvas bag.

Spike and I helped Reggie wrap the fuse bundles in newspaper and place them cautiously on top of the neatly stacked dynamite sticks.

Once the bag was filled, Reggie picked it up and eased the carrying strap over his left shoulder. With his bike resting against his right hip, he gently removed the canvas bag from around his shoulder and painstakingly stretched the carrying strap over the handlebars.

Straddling his bike, Reggie proclaimed, "Well, guys, I guess we're ready to head back to town. We sure as hell can't take this stuff home with us tonight, so we'll stash it in the drain pipe that runs along Highway 24. And, oh by the way, Spike, I ain't gonna be able to race you back to Harrington with this stuff ridin' up front. Some other time, huh?"

"That's okay, Reg. I wasn't gonna ride too close to ya, anyway. If you get hit by a semi, there's gonna be an awful big hole in the highway." Spike said smiling, seemingly satisfied with the way things were going.

As we neared the Erie viaduct, we crossed over the left lane of 24 and about 20 feet into the grassy strip that ran along the roadway. We laid down our bikes and walked the last 50 feet to the entrance of the 4-foot drain pipe. As the rest of us waited outside, Reggie carried the canvas bag into the circle of blackness.

Within 2 minutes, he reappeared at the entrance. Once outside of the drain pipe, Reggie straightened up to his full height, raised his hands to chest level and brushed his palms together several times, indicating the job was satisfactorily completed.

"The stuff should be safe in there," Reggie said reassuringly. "It's in there about 30 feet, where it's nice and dry and nobody can see it from the outside. Let's hope it don't rain tonight. Our stash could end up in the Wabash river."

Glancing at his watch, Reggie observed, "It's almost 4:30 now. Whadda ya say we call it quits for today, and we all meet back here at the drain pipe at 10:00 in the morning."

Spike and I quickly nodded our agreement. Pete and Wally, although more slowly and much less enthusiastically, also nodded in the affirmative. At that moment, they looked as if they'd just been given the death sentence.

Having completed the day's business, we all headed out in the direction of our homes, each mulling over his own thoughts as to what untold adventures tomorrow would bring.

I don't think any of us slept too well that night. In fact, I had a pretty terrifying nightmare that caused me to wake up screaming about 2:00 in the morning.

Wednesday morning dawned hot and humid. The wind picked up around 8:00 AM, and rapidly developing storm clouds indicated that a rainstorm was imminent.

Reggie and I rushed through our morning chores, motivated to new energy heights by the disturbing thought that our dynamite could be washed away in a flash flood. Mom's questioning looks indicated her puzzlement over our whirlwind pace.

Needless to say, we finished our chores in record time. At precisely 9:00 o'clock, we bid Mom a hurried good-bye and rushed out the front door, leaving her standing there with her hands on her hips. As we bounded down the front steps, the rain broke loose in buckets-full. We were drenched to the skin before we reached the street in front of our house.

Loud enough to be heard above the din of the storm, Reggie yelled frantically, "Kick it into high! We gotta save the dynamite."

Spurred to greater speeds than we thought ourselves capable, we plunged blindly ahead through the torrential downpour. As we sped down the hill past the Harrington Labs, slipping and sliding on the wet grass, I could feel myself slowing down under the weight of my saturated clothing. My tennis shoes were like super-soaked sponges, each one squirting water out the sides and making loud squishing sounds when contact was made with the ground.

By the time I reached Highway 24, Reggie was already out of sight, behind the wall of rain. I wondered how he could have even seen the on-coming traffic well enough to have crossed safely. I strained to see any headlights, took a deep breath, and then lunged off the curb and into the highway. Ten long, leaping steps and I was across safely.

As I neared the opening to the drain pipe, I could hear Reggie inside, sloshing his way toward me. The fast flowing water already looked to be about a foot deep inside the pipe.

Before I could see Reggie in the dark interior, I could hear him cursing. "Grab this damn bag, Mark. I had a helluva time findin' it."

As I peered into the pipe, straining to see Reggie, the wet canvas bag came flying out of the blackness, hitting me hard in the chest and almost knocking me down.

"What the hell do ya think your doin', Reg?" I screamed at him, as he stepped outside. "You scared the shit outta me. How would you like to be hit in the chest with a bag fulla of dynamite and blasting caps?"

"Don't get your bowels in an uproar!" he responded sarcastically. "That stuff is pretty safe the way it's wrapped and everything. Besides, I was gettin' tired of carryin' it. Geez, I had to feel my way down the pipe an extra hundred feet to find it. At the rate the current was movin', it woulda been in the big sewer pipe in another 5 minutes."

"Well, okay," I said apologetically, as I stood there holding the wet canvas bag. "I just never expected this thing to come flyin' outta nowhere at me. I nearly shit my pants. Anyway, as wet as this bag is, I doubt if the stuff'll work."

"Man, you don't know nothin' about dynamite, do ya?" Reggie responded impatiently. "Hell, they can use this stuff to blast under water."

"Here, give it to me," he said, yanking the bag from my hands. "We'll take it up on the Erie tracks and put it n that old tool crib the railroaders used to use."

As we started up the hill toward the railroad tracks, Reggie smiled at me and said, " Ya know, I think the storm is breakin' up. This may turn out to be a pretty good day after all."

The sun was breaking through the clouds as we started up the hill to the railroad track, and you could feel the heat again.

When we had reached the railroad-track level, we walked directly to the wooden, chest-type, tool crib.

Having stashed the bag inside the tool crib, Reggie turned and said, "Tell ya what. Let's go back down to 24, and wait for the guys at the Texaco station. I gotta dime. I can buy us a couple RC's while were waitin'."

I immediately began thinking how good that ice-cold RC was going to taste. Old Charlie Oberly kept his cold drinks buried in chipped ice that he hand-chipped from a 50-pound ice block. You could be sure that one of his frosty bottled drinks would be cold enough to literally take your breath away.

A few minutes later, we were enjoying our RC's in the sun, outside the service station. The first delicious swallow lived up to my expectations, prompting an involuntary "Ah-h-h-h". Reggie, looking at me, grinned broadly and said, "Purty damn good, huh?"

We had just finished our drinks when I spotted Wally about a block away. "Hey, Wally, over here at the station," I yelled.

Spike and Pete arrived a few minutes after Wally had joined us. Once we were all assembled in the station parking lot, Reggie filled the guys in on where the stash was and why it had been moved.

"Let's go get the stuff and get this show on the road," Reggie suggested.

The five of us headed up to the railroad tracks.

Having arrived at the tool crib once again, Reggie lifted the lid and pulled out the canvas bag. Before he had fully lowered the lid, Spike was nudging him with his elbow to get his attention.

Spike, who was wide-eyed with fright, could only mutter, "Uh-uh-uh-uh," as pointed down the tracks.

Reggie spun around and looked in the direction Spike was pointing. "Holy shit, it's old Cap Jenkins the Railroad Dick, and he's got his pit bull!" Reggie exclaimed. "Let's get the hell outta here!"

We were all terror-struck at the prospect of being caught by Cap.

Cap Jenkins was the Erie Railroad Detective. He was a huge, bellicose man, who enjoyed nothing better than busting the heads of the hoboes he found on railroad property. It was rumored that some years before, during the depression, he had been responsible for a couple of deaths.

As we began running down the tracks, a couple hundred feet in front of Cap, we heard his booming voice calling, "You boys stop right where you are. I wanna talk to you."

We responded by running even faster.

It felt as if an electric shock shot up my spine when I heard Cap bark, "Go get 'em, Blackie!" He had unleashed his pit bull!

Reggie, who was running slightly ahead, looked back over his shoulder and yelled, "Head for the college woods, guys. It's our only chance!"

For an instant, I looked back over my shoulder and quickly determined the big black dog with the mean red eyes was gaining ground fast. My heart felt as if it would leap from my chest.

"Get to other side of the crick!" Reggie yelled, as he suddenly swerved sharply left and started sliding down the muddy embankment toward the creek. The rest of us were about 50 feet behind Reggie when he jumped feet-first into the fast-moving, chest-deep water. He held tightly to the canvas bag slung over his shoulder, as he struggled against the current to reach the other side of the creek.

The rest of us were just reaching the water's edge as Reggie pulled himself up onto the far bank. Wally, as usual, was bringing up the rear, and the barking dog was right on his heels.

Spike, Pete, and I were already in the water when Wally reached the edge of the creek. As Wally hesitated at water's edge, the snarling attack dog leaped down the embankment and landed on Wally's back, almost knocking him in the water.

In an instant, the dog had a bone-crushing hold on the lower part of Wally's left leg. Wally was screaming obscenities as he engaged in a deadly tug-of-war with this monster of a dog.

As the rest of us watched the melee in horror from the other bank, Reggie yelled frantically, "Kick the son-of-a-bitch with your other foot, Wally!"

Wally, on his back and resting on his elbows, drew back his right foot, and plunged his heel forward with all his strength. Solid contact was made with the large black head, and the dog momentarily lost its grip on Wally's leg. Wally, with his leg free, scrambled into water and started swimming toward the rest of us.

The dog, who had been momentarily stunned, stood up, shook his head, and then leaped into the water.

We had just pulled Wally out of the water, when we saw that the dog was in trouble. The swift current was too much for the dog and was taking him downstream.

As we headed into the concealment of the woods, we could hear Cap Jenkins bellowing from the railroad embankment, "What did you bastards do with my dog? If I ever catch ya, I'll kill ya!"

In a safe area deep inside the woods, we stopped and rested.

As we sat there under a big oak tree, Wally was the first to speak. "Man, I thought my 'my ass was grass', he commented breathlessly.

"Here, let me take a look at your leg," Reggie said, looking at Wally.

Wally pulled the left leg of his jeans up to the knee, revealing a nasty set of teeth marks on the calf of his leg. The skin was leaking a little blood around some of teeth punctures and was already puffy and beginning to turn a purplish red color.

"Don't seem too bad too me," Reggie observed matter-of-factly. "Didn't even have time to draw much blood. Boy, you were luckier than hell. They say that when one of them pits gets a hold of ya, they never let go."

"Yeah, you were purty damn lucky, Wally," Spike conceded. "He could still be crunching on that leg bone. Does it hurt much?"

"It's beginin' to throb some, but I think I'll be okay." Wally replied.

"I wonder if that ol' dog made it." I commented.

"Who gives a shit," Spike said contemptuously. "I just hope ol' Cap didn't get a good look at us."

"I don't think he ever got close enough to see our faces," Pete remarked.

"Well, guys, are we still gonna try out the dynamite today?" Reggie asked.

With a look of total disdain, Spike shot back, "That's what we're here for, ain't it?"

"Well, I don't know if it's such a good idea now," Wally whined. "After what's happened already, it don't seem like a very good day."

"I think we oughta hold off, too." Pete said, looking very worried.

"Well, I think you guys are a couple of chicken-shits," Spike said scornfully, "and I vote we go ahead as planned."

"I'll hafta second that vote," Reggie conceded. "We don't know what the weather's gonna be like for the rest of the week, and today's turnin' out purty good."

"I guess I'll hafta go with Reg and Spike," I said, out of loyalty to Reggie.

"Well, the majority rules," Reggie observed. "I think that sandy beach upstream from the Clay Banks would be a good place to experiment. Besides, hardly anybody but us ever goes that far back in the woods."

About 5 minutes later, we arrived at the place along the creek that Reggie had chosen. As the rest of us stood and watched without saying a word, Reggie laid the canvas bag on the ground and carefully removed a stick of dynamite and a fuse.

As Reggie pulled out his pocket knife, he began to speak. "I don't think we oughta use a full stick the first time. Ya see, ya can actually cut off any amount ya want to."

He laid the 6-inch dynamite stick on a flat rock and began sawing on it. It was apparent that I wasn't the only one who was apprehensive, as we all quickly moved back to a point 40 to 50 feet away from Reggie.

"Reg, I don't think that's a very good idea," I said in a trembling voice.

"It's okay, Mark. I've seen Uncle Art do this before," he said reassuringly, in a measured voice.

"See, no problem," he said proudly, as he laid the pieces down. "The next step is to insert the fuse-cap end of the fuse into the dynamite," he droned on.

With the fuse in one hand and the 2-inch piece of dynamite in the other, he pushed the copper fuse cap into the end of the dynamite stub. Completing that phase, he looked back to where the rest of us were huddled together, and inquired calmly, "Any of you guys got some dry matches. Mine are still purty wet."

Without a word, Spike reached into his pocket and withdrew a book of matches, and threw them Frisbee-style to Reggie. The matches landed at Reggie's feet.

The rest of us stood mesmerized by the scene that was unfolding.

With the matches in his left hand and the fused dynamite in his other, Reggie walked about 20 feet to the edge of the creek, where he laid the dynamite and matches aside and began burrowing into the soft, wet sand with his cupped hands. When he had scooped out sufficient sand to form a hole approximately 8 inches wide and 10 inches deep, he placed the small stick of dynamite into the bottom of the hole. Leaving about 18 inches of the yellow cord-like fuse protruding from the top of hole, he filled the hole with sand.

Having neatly patted down the sand on the surface, Reggie picked up the matches, tore one from the book, and struck it on the outside cover. He then quickly picked up the fuse end and laid the flaming match against it. Almost immediately sparks began to emanate from the fuse.

"Fire in the hole!" he yelled loudly, as he dropped the lit fuse and sprinted to our location.

He stood over us smiling, with his hands on his hips, as he surveyed the quivering huddle before him.

I guess we were quite a sight; on our knees, bent forward with our foreheads to the ground, and clasping our hands behind our heads, using the protective posture the Sisters of St. Matthews had taught us for surviving an enemy air attack.

"Geez, guys, what are ya expectin'? A 500-pound bomb, or somethin'?" Reggie asked derisively. "You're a safe distance away. Besides, ya need to be sittin' up so ya can see the full effects. Hell, it's gonna be about 5 minutes till it goes off, anyway. So sit up and enjoy the fireworks."

We all got up a little sheepishly and sat there on ground, staring in the direction of the sparks that moved inexorably toward the mound of sand.

Finally, the sparks disappeared beneath the sand. Less than a minute later, "Kaboom!" The earth shook beneath us, and a large, dense cloud of sandy particles rose 50 feet in the air.

There was a long silence as we sat there wide-eyed, looking at one another. As the sand fell out of the air, some of it landed on our heads.

When the sand cloud finally settled to the ground, all that remained was a smoking hole 3 feet across and 2 feet deep where the dynamite had been originally planted. At that time, I think we all appreciated the destructive power of that little 2-inch stick of dynamite.

The acrid smoke stung our eyes and nostrils, as we walked slowly to the blast site to survey the damage.

As we stood there looking down at the hole, Spike said excitedly, "Ya know what, fellas? This is just like them demolition guys in the armed forces. You know, them Navy UDT guys and the Army Rangers. Those guys getta blow the hell outta everything. This shit makes me feel like John Wayne in one a them war movies. Reg, can I be the one to try the dynamite next?"

"Yeah, I don't see why not." Reggie replied. "But I think for our next experiment, we oughta take out a tree stump, and that's gonna take more than a 2-inch stick. Tell ya what, why don't we just use the 4-inch piece left over from that last blast?"

"Sounds good to me," Spike responded enthusiastically. "What say we go find me a stump?"

We began walking south, along the main path that followed the creek, all eyes searching the area for a likely demolition candidate. The main path had turned uphill and we had progressed to a point high above the creek, only a few hundred feet from the Clay Banks.

Pete, who was about 10 feet to the rear of Wally, finally broke the silence. "Hey, Wally, start runnin' and see if I can hit ya with this 'hocker' I just coughed up."

"Like hell I will!" Wally exclaimed, glancing back over his shoulder apprehensively.

"C'mon, Wally," Pete pleaded. I don't wanna waste this 'pearly' (Pete's name for a sizeable glob of mucous that had taken on a greenish-gray hue)".

"Hell, I'm givin' ya a runnin' start." Pete said, sounding a little agitated. "If ya don't start runnin' now, I'm gonna hafta let ya have it where ya stand."

Wally, the terror now showing in his eyes, took off at a dead run.

Pete's cheeks were undulating as he worked his mouth to bring the giant wad forward to the launching position.

We all stood and watched admiringly as the master went to work. Pete was famous for his hockers — not only the size and glue-like consistency of the missiles, but also his unerring accuracy.

The tip of Pete's tongue was now projected beyond his mouth, and his trademark firing mechanism — the curled sides of the tongue forming a tube, much like a beanshooter — was in evidence.

Wally was nearly forty feet in front when Pete took a deep breath and launched his missile. As the hocker exited Pete's mouth, it made a "Thwoot" sound, not unlike a dart leaving a pigmy's blowgun.

We watched the giant glob of sputum arc high in the air and roll end over end as it closed on Wally's fading form.

"Splat!" The gooey projectile found its target, as it pounded into the back of Wally's head with such force that Wally stumbled forward, falling to his knees.

Most of the slimy substance was embedded in Wally's hair and beginning to hang on strings down to his neckline.

"Awesome!" Spike exclaimed in admiration.

Wally was still on knees, wiping the back of his head with dried leaves, when he looked up at Pete and screamed, "You dirty asshole!" "Next time, find somebody else to be your damn target. I think I'm gonna be sick."

Once we stopped laughing, we were able to continue down the main path, in search of a stump.

We stopped abruptly, when Pete yelled, "Hey, fellas, over here!" "How 'bout this one?" he said, pointing to a huge, dead tree that leaned out over the steep embankment that ran down to the creek.

We all walked over to the edge of the incline and surveyed the old tree. Its roots were nearly all exposed due to the erosion underneath, where great quantities of earth had given way and slid down the steep bank and into the creek. The exposed root system formed a natural roof above the area where the bank had eroded away from the tree. Only about a third of the roots still remained anchored in the solid ground.

"Well, Pete, that ain't exactly a stump," Reggie observed, "But, ta tell the truth, you may've come up with somethin' even better. The way I figger, a charge under them ol' roots oughta send that baby all the way down to the crick. Do ya think you're ready, Spike?"

"Hell, I ain't never been readier," Spike responded. "Gimme the dynamite."

Reggie handed Spike the 4-inch piece of dynamite, a 5-minute fuse, and the book of matches, warning, "Now, be damn careful, Spike. If ya get in trouble, give a yell, and I'll try to help ya. Meanwhile, the rest of us will wait down the path a ways."

Spike, with the fuse coiled over his shoulder and the dynamite stick in his hip pocket, walked to the base of the old tree and used the big root system as a ladder to descend beneath the tree. He soon disappeared under the ledge at the base of the tree.

Minutes passed and not a word from Spike. We were all getting pretty nervous.

Finally, Pete yelled, "Everything okay down there, Spike?"

A frightened voice responded, "I'm in trouble down here, guys! My foot's caught in the roots and the fuse is burnin'. I—I—I—I can't get loose and don't know how much time I got!"

Reggie ran to the edge of the bank and peered down. "Holy Shit! He's hangin' by one foot and I can't even see the dynamite!" he yelled back at the rest of us. "I gotta go get 'im," he said resignedly, as he crouched down to start his descent.

In an instant, Wally bolted from our midst and ran toward the ominous scene. Before Reggie could start his climb down the roots, Wally was in back of him, grabbing him by the shoulders, and throwing him back on the seat of his pants.

Reggie sat there in utter amazement, as he watched Wally flash by him, climb over the embankment's edge, and begin clambering down the roots.

As soon as Reggie gained his composure, he moved to the edge and peered down into the root system. He could see Wally, working his way toward Spike.

"Whadda ya think you're doin', Wally!" Reggie yelled.

"I'm gonna get Spike outta here," Wally responded matter-of-factly.

"No! First, just get the dynamite and throw it down the hill," Reggie barked. "Then ya worry about gettin' Spike out."

"I can see the fuse burnin', but I can't reach the dynamite, Reg!" Wally yelled back. "Spike threw it too far back in the crevice, and I don't think there's much fuse left! What'll I do?"

"You're gonna hafta get his foot loose!" Reggie screamed. "Should I come down?"

"Stay there!" Wally shouted. "There's not enough time! She's gonna blow any second!"

From his vantage point, Reggie could see Wally, hanging by one hand from a root, with his pocket knife in the other hand, sawing furiously at the shoe laces of Spike's entrapped foot.

Spike, wide-eyed with fear, could only hang there upside-down, his life literally in Wally's hands. I'm certain he was also stunned at the thought of Wally being capable of such an heroic act. And maybe, just maybe, he was wishing he could retract all of the miserable things he had done and said to Wally in the past.

Suddenly the shoe laces parted, and Spike's foot slid out of his shoe, launching him into a head-first free-fall. He landed hard on Wally, and the two of them tumbled together down the steep embankment.

Waiting just long enough to see Spike extricated, Reggie immediately began a mad dash in our direction. He had progressed no more than 20 feet when the thunderous explosion occurred. "Ka-woomph!" The concussion knocked Reggie in the air, flipping him completely head-over-heels and depositing him on his butt and elbows about 10 feet in front of the rest of us.

Reggie, appearing somewhat stunned, got to his feet quickly and looked in the direction of the old tree, which had already begun to tilt acutely in the direction of Spike and Wally.

As the tree fell with a mighty crash, we all ran to the edge of embankment.

Spike was pulling Wally out the creek, when he looked up to see the big tree plummeting toward them. He was barely able to leap out of the way of massive limbs as they spun wildly by him, making a loud whooshing sound. Wally was not so lucky. We lost sight of him for an instant as the limbs engulfed him.

An instant later, the big tree landed in the creek with a tidal-wave-like splash.

The aftermath was chaotic, with Spike running toward Wally's lifeless form, which lay half in and half out of the water at the creek's edge.

We could now see the blood pooling up on the surface of the water, as we stumbled down the embankment to give what assistance we could.

My heart was pounding uncontrollably, and I was finding it hard to breath, as we neared the spot where Wally laid.

Spike, with tears streaming down his face, was bent over Wally's inert body, calling his name.

Spike was abruptly brought to his senses when he heard Reggie yell, "Is he breathin', Spike? For Christ's sakes, is he breathin'?"

Spike immediately fell to his knees, and bending forward, placed his right ear in the proximity of Wally's nose and mouth.

The rest of us stood in silence, unable to help as we watched Spike, who was choking on his tears and frantically seeking some sign of life in his unlikely benefactor.

After what seemed to be an eternity, Spike exploded to his feet, startling the rest of us. "I think I heard him groan!" he screamed giddily.

Reggie got down on the ground beside Spike and gently lifted Wally's head in the crook of his arm. "Can ya hear me, Wally?" he pleaded.

"U-h-h-h-h," was the response, and Wally's eyelids flickered slightly and then slowly opened.

Wally had a confused look as he peered up at Reggie. Above his left eye was an ugly, blue bump. The only other visible injury was a 3-inch gash above his right ankle, which was bleeding freely.

"What happened?" Wally said haltingly. "Oh, now I remember. Did I get Spike out okay?"

"Yeah, Spike's just fine." Reggie said reassuringly. "He's right there on the other side of ya."

Wally turned his head slowly to see Spike's smiling face.

"Wally, ya did a great thing. I wouldn't be here if it wasn't for you. I owe ya, buddy," Spike said gratefully, wiping his eyes with his forearm.

"We better do somethin' about that cut on your leg, Wally," Reggie said. It's not bleedin' as bad as it was, but it looks purty deep. Okay, guys, gimme all your clean handkerchiefs. We gotta get this thing bandaged up."

We were able to come up with three seemingly sanitary handkerchiefs, with which Reggie proceeded to dress Wally's leg wound.

"Are you hurtin' any place beside that cut on your leg and the bump on your head?" Spike asked.

"Well, the ribs on my right side are purty sore," Wally acknowledged, " and I'm a little dizzy from gettin' conked on the head, too. I guess that's about it."

"Well, one thing's for sure. Wally ain't gonna be walkin' back to Harrington," Reggie mused.

"You guys help me get him up to the railroad tracks, and I'll carry him the rest of the way," Spike quickly responded.

"You're not goin' anywhere without this, Spike," Pete said, handing Spike his missing shoe. "It was still lodged in the roots of that old tree."

"Thanks, Pete," Spike said grinning. "Hell, I'd forgot all about that. Guess I woulda remembered once I got up on the tracks and tried to walk on them stones."

All four of us struggled to carry Wally up the steep embankment. Once on the railroad tracks, we sat on the wooden ties to rest a few minutes.

"Okay, fellas, we'd better start back," Reggie suggested. "Are you up ta ridin' on Spike's back, Wally?"

"Yeah, I think so," came Wally's reply.

As Spike crouched down, Reggie and I lifted Wally onto Spike's back. With Wally riding piggy-back style on his back, Spike straightened up and began walking laboriously down the cinder path, along the railroad tracks. The rest of us followed, spreading out along the railroad tracks, a few feet above the cinder path.

After a short distance, Reggie reached out and patted Pete on the shoulder, saying, "I'm damn glad you remembered to pick up the bag of dynamite." "I can take it now," he said, as he removed it from Pete's shoulder.

"What are we gonna do with the stuff now?" Pete asked. "Personally, I don't care if I ever see dynamite agin."

"You may be right, Pete," Reggie conceded. "Maybe we oughta shitcan this stuff. I'm beginin' to feel real creepy just carryin' it around."

We had progressed about a quarter-mile, when Reggie asked, "Ya want me to take 'im for awhile, Spike?"

"Naw, he ain't heavy, Reg. He's my buddy." Spike replied, giggling.

"Man, I stepped into that one, didn't I?" Reggie said, feigning disgust. "Didn't they use a line somethin' like that in "Boys Town"? Hell, you were just waitin' for a chance to use it, weren't cha?" he asked, a big smile spreading across his face.

"Why do you ask, oh most reverend Father Flannigan?" Spike responded devilishly, in his best Irish brogue.

The rest of us broke into uncontrolled laughter.

The day had certainly surpassed all of our expectations.

On the way back to our homes that day, we voted unanimously to get rid of the remaining dynamite. Apparently, we were all anxious to conclude that phase of our lives.

The old canvas bag and its contents were stashed deep inside an old hollow tree. The hole at the base of the tree was then filled with sticks and leaves, in an effort to conceal the deadly cache forever. It may still be there today.

Wally's leg required eight stitches, and it kept him hobbled for a couple of days. Of course, his mom and dad never knew the real details of his injury.

I believe Wally considered his wound a badge of honor and seemed to thoroughly enjoy his new-found status as a hero.

From that time on, it seemed that Spike couldn't do enough for Wally. They were the closest of buddies and did everything together.

The Beat Goes On

The rest of the Easter vacation was somewhat less noteworthy than the first few days.

We did, however, have a little adventure on Sunday, the day before we returned to school.

It had rained torrents during the period of Thursday through Saturday. Flooding was widespread throughout the Harrington area.

On Sunday morning, after returning home from early mass, Reggie, Spike, and I decided to roam around and check out the storm's aftermath.

The rivers and creeks had over-flowed their banks, and many homes had been flooded. A large number of homes along the Wabash River had to be evacuated, and the families were being cared for in the Central School gymnasium until the waters subsided. The devastating effects of the water were evident everywhere, and our hearts went out to the people who had temporarily lost their homes.

Aside from the devastation, there was a place in our neighborhood that especially intrigued the three of us.

An empty property two blocks from the Gearing house was under eight to ten feet of water. The three-lot property was formed by a natural depression at the corner of Kimmel and Cottage Streets.

Someone in our group suggested that we ask Mr. Burke, a neighbor, to borrow his fishing boat and take it for a cruise on our newly discovered lake.

Mr. Burke was surprisingly obliging, but cautioned us that we'd be responsible for any damage and that the boat must be returned by 4 o'clock that afternoon.

The tough part of the proposition was transporting this heavy, old boat to its destination, nearly three blocks away.

We somehow managed to carry, drag, and scoot the heavy, wooden boat to the water hole.

We positioned the boat so its bow was pointed down the bank, about three feet from the water's edge. It was at that moment that we realized the problem: the bank was too steep and the water too deep for one us to be able to shove the boat away from the bank and still be able to join the other two inside. We needed a fourth person to launch us — one who would not be part of the crew.

As we stood there on the bank, puzzling over our problem, our solution was about to arrive on the scene. About a block south on Cottage Street, we could see a familiar, but generally unwelcome form moving toward us.

George Wearly, the neighborhood bully, most likely returning home from church, had already caught sight of us and his pace quickened noticeably.

"Oh, oh, here comes trouble," Reggie said nervously, as he mulled over in his mind his last encounter with George.

In their last meeting, George, who was two years older than Reggie and about a head taller, grabbed Reggie on his way to school and demanded any money he might be carrying. On this occasion, Reggie was able to break away by punching George hard in the stomach, then running the rest of the way to school.

Reggie remembered vividly the scene of George, doubled over in pain, screaming vile threats of what he'd do the next time he saw Reggie.

"I don't think he's got the guts to try somethin' with the three of us here," Reggie mused.

"Just let 'im try. He'll get his ass kicked," Spike said boastfully.

George came to a stop about ten feet from us. "What are you punks up to?" he demanded menacingly, glaring down at us, with his feet spread wide and his hands on his hips.

Reggie seemed to catch George off guard when he responded, "How ya doin', George? Long time, no see."

George, looking really puzzled and a lot less angry, asked, "Are you guys tryin' to put that boat in the water?"

"Man, you hit the nail right on the head, George," Reggie said friendly-like. "You wouldn't consider shovin' us off, would ya, old buddy?"

"Well, a-a-a. Yeah, I guess so," George replied hesitantly.

At that, the three of us piled into boat.

The boat had already begun to slide down the muddy bank toward the water, when George placed his hands on the stern and began pushing hard.

As the boat floated rapidly away from the bank, we looked back, in the direction of the loud cursing. George had slid down the muddy bank on the seat his pants and was now waist deep in water, yelling obscenities.

"I just ruined my Sunday suit! I'm gonna make you little bastards pay the next time I catch ya!" He bellowed, as he stood there, all red in the face, and shaking his fist at us.

"Aw, blow it out your ass, George!" Spike yelled back defiantly, while giving him a one-finger salute.

Reggie and I were laughing hysterically, making us almost too weak to pull hard enough on the oars to put us a safe distance from George.

We looked back one more time to see George standing on the bank, trying in vain to hit us with rocks.

We had spent several wonderful hours paddling around the water hole, pretending to be everything from pirates to PT boat sailors.

It was about 3 o'clock in the afternoon, and we were getting real tired, when we saw Dad's '37 Chevy pulling along side the curb at Cottage Street. He didn't look too happy when he waved for us to come to the shore.

"What the hell are you boys doin' out there in that deep water!" he yelled, as we approached the shore. "And where did ya get that boat?" he demanded.

"Geez, Dad, we just borrowed it from Mr. Burke for a little while, so we could take a little cruise before the water goes down," Reggie replied contritely.

"Well, your sailin' days are over. You can cruise your asses back to Mr. Burke's right now, while the boat's still in one piece," Dad said gruffly, as he helped pull the boat up the bank.

"But, Dad, we're too tired to carry the boat back now," Reggie pleaded.

"Then I guess I'll hafta give you guys a little help," Dad responded, the irritation showing in his voice. "Flip the boat over, and hook the bow on my back bumper. While I drive, you three boys can carry the stern."

Dad climbed into car and waited for us. In response to his direction, we lifted the inverted bow-end of the boat up and hooked it over the two vertical members of the car's back bumper. Then the three of us went to the rear of the boat and lifted the stern in the air. With the car supporting the front of the boat, we three were equally displaced across the stern-end; Reggie in the middle, and Spike and I each manning one side.

Even with help from Dad's car, the old boat still felt like a ton of dead weight.

"Are you guys ready back there?" Dad yelled impatiently.

"Yeah, I guess so," Reggie replied.

"Well, here we go!" Dad said matter-of-factly.

At the instant the car surged forward, I glanced into the rear window and caught Dad's reflection in the rear-view mirror. He was smiling devilishly.

At first, we only had to walk at a fast pace to keep up. But I guess Dad, who kept watching us in the rear-view mirror, was not satisfied that this was fast enough. So he pushed the accelerator down a couple more notches, until he had us on a dead run.

Panic had set in for the three of us. We were not only running as fast as we could to keep up, our fingers were now beginning to throb from the weight of the old boat.

After two blocks, our hands and forearms were so numb we could no longer feel them. Our lungs were beginning to burn, as we sucked in as much oxygen as we could.

The fast pace caused our legs to be involuntarily jerked into making abnormally giant strides. It didn't take much of this before our thighs felt as though they would ignite.

At one point, Dad yelled out the window, "Whatever you do, don't drop that boat! We can't afford to pay for that damn thing!"

As the car started down the steep grade of Finley, it was clear that Spike was in terrible shape. "I can't hold on any longer," he pleaded, tears welling up in his eyes.

"Dammit, Spike, you heard what Dad said!" Reggie barked. "Ya gotta hang on! There's only two blocks to go.

We finally reached the bottom of Finley Street and were starting up the hill.

My arms felt like they had left their shoulder sockets.

Spike was sobbing incoherently, but still holding on.

Dad finally applied the brakes as the car drew even with Mr. Burke's driveway.

The suddenness of the car braking caused the three of us to fly forward against the stern panel, momentarily knocking the air out of us.

When Dad finally stopped the car in the driveway, we immediately dropped our burden to the ground, leaving the bow of the boat still attached to the bumper. It was all we could do to stagger to the side of the driveway and collapse in the grass.

Dad, having walked around the rear of the car, peered down at us, smiling.

We were oblivious to his presence and just laid there, gasping for air and moaning in agony.

"How ya doin', fellas? Havin' a good time?" he asked sarcastically.

"Are you kiddin'?" Reggie said, staring up in amazement. "Geez, you coulda killed us, Dad."

"Well, do you think you learned anything today?" Dad asked.

"Yeah, the next time, we won't let you help us return the boat," Reggie replied, smiling mischievously. "I'm only kiddin', Dad. We learned our lesson. That was a dangerous thing we did today. And we shouldn't go around borrowin' our neighbor's stuff."

"I think you boys will know better than to pull this kind of stunt in the future," Dad said. "Now put the boat back by the garage and I'll take you home."

The next day, Monday, we were back in school at St. Matthew's. It was difficult settling back into the routine of school, after having such an exciting Easter vacation. Fortunately, it was only a little over a month before we finished our school year and began summer vacation.

We had many good times that summer — swimming, fishing, and playing slips in the College Woods — but one day stands out in my memory: August 14, 1945, V-J Day, the day that Japan surrendered, ending World War II.

Happiness reigned that day. It seemed that everyone in Harrington gravitated to the downtown area to join in the mass celebration.

Convoys of cars, with horns blaring, circled the shopping district. Several of the local fire engines cruised the same route with their sirens screaming. People on the sidewalks were cheering. Total strangers were hugging and kissing one another.

At first the five of us — Reggie, Spike, Pete, Wally, and I — could only stand around marveling at the spectacle. But it wasn't long before we joined in the festivities.

Like a lot of other people, we hitched a ride on one of the fire engines. After we tired of that ride, we mingled with people on the street.

Spike came up with an activity that proved to be the most fun of all. Since some of the prettiest girls in town were being grabbed and kissed, Spike decided to get in on the action.

After one very attractive girl had just been kissed by a sailor, Spike made his move. As the sailor released her and stepped back, Spike slid in between them and planted a big sloppy kiss on the girl's lips. The fact that this voluptuous young lady was at least four years Spike's senior and a head taller didn't intimidate him one bit.

Having successfully stolen his kiss, Spike quickly ducked into crowd and ran to join the rest of us. The girl was left there standing with a shocked look. It is not surprising that after that Spike was really strutting his stuff.

Having been shown the way, the rest of us tried our hands at stealing kisses, the ultimate thievery.

Some of the town merchants stood in front of their stores and handed out snacks and drinks. Needless to say, we always took full advantage of any thing free.

As we drew close to the town's most popular tobacco store, we observed the proprietor handing out cigars to all the men. Reggie, in his inimitable style, sneaked through the crowd to a position behind the store owner and grabbed a handful of cigars from one of the open boxes.

We must have been quite a sight, each of us puffing on a big, black cigar, jauntily held in the corner of our mouths.

Unfortunately, the cigars were our undoing that day. It wasn't long before each of us seemed to turn a different shade of green.

The alley behind the buildings became our refuge when we could no longer hold down all the hot dogs and pop we had consumed.

We stayed back in the alley until each of us had his turn at upchucking.

We were all still feeling pretty miserable when we finally walked out of the alley. It was at this time that Spike uttered one of his more memorable "pearls of wisdom": "I don't know about you fellas, but I think I'm gonna pass up them black stogies in the future."

For a number of years thereafter, the very smell of a cigar instantly brought back the queasiness I had experienced on V-J day.

One of our favorite pastimes that summer was engaging in rubber-gun fights. It was with these weapons that we could reenact some of the more fierce WWII battles of the South Pacific.

A rubber gun was a device constructed from a rectangular piece of lumber; a large nail; an old-fashion, two-prong wooden clothes pin; and the main ingredient — several strips of rubber inner-tubing, which were used as large rubber bands.

The main purpose of the completed gun was to hold taut a fully stretched, 1/2-inch-wide, nearly 2-foot long rubber band until the shooter released the rubber projectile in the direction of his target.

It should be noted that inner tubes in those days were the inflatable donuts that were used inside car tires to provide the necessary rigidity needed for a cushioned ride.

Synthetic-rubber inner tubes, which were used as a replacement for the pre-war rubber variety, were plentiful during the war years. Unfortunately, the synthetic material lacked the stretchability that was required for the manufacture of a quality rubber gun. Only the pre-war rubber inner tube would do, and in the summer of 1945, they were all but extinct.

Reggie and I felt we had "Hit it Rich" when Spike appeared at our front door one morning with two old, red-rubber inner tubes, one slung over each shoulder.

"Whadda ya think, fellas?" he asked, grinning broadly.

"Geez, that's enough rubber for ten or twelve guns," Reggie replied excitedly. "Mark, get on the phone and round up Pete, Wally, and Dan. Tell 'em we're gonna be makin' some rubber guns."

While Reggie and Spike went out to search for the other materials in Dad's shed, I began making the phone calls.

Having notified the other three guys of our plans, I waited in the house until they arrived, and then immediately escorted them to the shed.

Inside the shed, Reggie and Spike had already rounded up all the necessary tools and materials to complete the project, even the wooden clothes pins, pilfered from Mom's clothesline bag.

We all sat down on the concrete floor and set to work fashioning our own personal weapons.

The basis of a good rubber gun was the wooden stock, a piece of wood most commonly cut from a 1-by-6-inch board. The rectangular piece of wood could vary from 18 to 24 inches in length. Since the object was to stretch the rubber bands lengthwise around the wood, the longer the stock of the gun was, the more powerful the weapon would be.

After the wooden stock was completed, a large nail was partially driven into the wood about 2 inches from the bottom corner that would be nearest the shooter's hand. Positioned in this fashion, the nail would act as the trigger-pull mechanism.

Next, one prong of the old-fashion, two-prong wooden clothes pin was broken off. The modified clothes pin became the hammer of the weapon.

Rubber bands were used to provide the gun's firing mechanism with the required spring tension, as well as to serve as ammunition for the gun. Scissors were used to cut the half-inch cross sections from the inner tube.

The step portion of the clothes pin, where the prong had been broken off, was placed against the rear edge of the stock so as to mesh with the bottom corner of the stock nearest the shooter. With the remaining prong pointing upward and its inside edge snugly against the rear edge of the stock, two rubber bands were stretched in parallel-fashion around the clothes pin and over the front edge of the stock. In this way, the flat side of the clothes pin was held firmly to the back edge of the wooden stock (the butt of the gun).

To load the rubber gun, another rubber band was pinched together at one end, and the pinched portion was pushed securely into the V-shaped notch formed by the mating surfaces of the top-inside portion of the clothes pin and the back edge of stock. The free end of the rubber band was then stretched tautly over the front end of the stock.

The shooter could then hold the loaded weapon with the knob-end of the old-type clothes pin resting against the crook of his hand and his forefinger hooked around the nail (the trigger mechanism). With his shooting hand positioned thusly, he could sight along the top edge of the wooden stock.

When the shooter had the target of his choice in his sight, he would squeeze on the trigger to fire the weapon. The squeezing motion of his hand caused the bottom of the clothes pin to move toward the trigger and the top prong of the clothes pin, in a pivoting reaction, to be moved away from the back edge of the stock. This pivoting action caused the V-shaped notch between the prong (hammer) and the gun stock to open, thus releasing the pinched end of the stretched rubber band. The sudden release of the rubber band caused it to be projected forward with great velocity. Within a range of 30 feet, the gun could deliver its rubber projectile with stinging force.

It was customary that after every rubber-gun battle, we would stand around and compare the ugly red welts that were symbolic of our war wounds. I must admit that the majority of our 'wounds' was to our posteriors, which was all that was available to our attackers as we threw down our empty guns and fled in panic.

Although it was considered illegal to shoot at the head and face of our opponents, it was acceptable to tie knots in the rubber loops to increase the pain potential.

After everyone had constructed their weapon, it was decided that we would go to the meadow to conduct some war games. So shortly after completing our weapon-making project, we started out eagerly in the direction of Erie tracks, each of us proudly carrying his brand-new rubber gun and six rounds of the rubber-band ammo.

As we walked along the railroad tracks on our way to the meadow, an occasional yelp would be heard as someone felt the sting of a well-aimed rubber band. I guess we felt compelled to get in some shooting practice before we reached the meadow, where the real battles would be played out.

The meadow was a fenced-in, 40-acre field, which was located on the east side of the Erie Railroad tracks and directly across from the northern limits of the College Woods. The flat grassy area lay about 50 feet below the Erie tracks, in a hollow formed by the raised railroad property on the west side and a natural 80-foot high plateau formation on the east side.

The rectangularly shaped meadow was fairly clear, except for a few small trees and thorn bushes. It was a perfect place for our team games, which included Capture the Flag, re-enactments of WWII battles, and, on occasion in the autumn, a good game of sandlot football.

A fence ran along the top of the hill on the east side of the meadow. On the other side of the fence and on top of the plateau formation, was a large pastureland where a herd of cows grazed daily.

Within 20 minutes of leaving our house, we had reached our destination. Once we had climbed over the barbed-wire-topped fence and were inside the boundaries of the meadow, Reggie gathered us together, saying, "Fall in over here, guys. We need to get these war games on the road. So does anybody have any ideas on whose gonna be fightin' who?"

As the rest of us were deep in thought, Spike jumped out in front, exclaiming, "I got the perfect answer. Reg and me will be the Generals of the two armies and we'll each choose two soldiers."

"Sounds fair to me," Reggie responded. "Pete, flip a coin to see which one of us gets to choose first."

Pete took a new-looking quarter from his pocket and while holding it balanced atop his right thumb nail, he turned toward Reggie and said, "Okay, Reg, call it in the air." An instant later, the coin shot upward off Pete's thumb.

As the silver coin spun rapidly into the air, rays of sun light flashed out from its shiny edges. Reggie, gazing skyward at the shiny object, finally called out, "Gimme heads!"

All eyes followed the quarter's descent as it came to rest in Pete's right palm, at which instant he brought his left palm over on top of his right palm, keeping the coin concealed from the rest of us. Purposely keeping us in suspense as long as he could, he raised his left hand slightly and peeked underneath. Finally turning toward Reggie, he smiled impishly and said, "Well, I guess you choose first, Reg."

Without hesitation, Reggie declared, "Mark'll be my First Lieutenant."

Fairly confident that he would consider picking me first, I still felt a rush of pride as I walked to his side.

Spike, his brow furrowed in concentration, studied the remaining three members intently. After 30 seconds or so, he abruptly declared with a smile, "Pete, you're gonna be my number one man."

Pete had taken no more than two steps in Spike's direction when Reggie announced his third and final selection, "C'mon over here and join the winners, Dan."

Wally, never looking up, walked slowly toward Spike and Pete. As he joined their side, he kicked angrily at a big clod of dirt and said forlornly, "Geez, you guys always pick me last. I'm gettin' sick of it."

"Aw, don't take it so personal, Wally," Pete said, as he draped his arm over Wally's shoulder. "Hell, now's your chance to prove yourself on the field of battle. Who knows, you may even win the Medal of Honor," he said, chuckling.

"Okay, enough of this chit-chat," Reggie interrupted. Pointing to the south, he began to lay out the game rules, "Spike, you take your men down that way about 300 feet and we'll face-off until I give the signal to charge. Any guy hit three times is considered dead and must stay where he was last shot. You can keep pickin' up ammo off the ground. Anybody that surrenders or is caught without ammo becomes a prisoner-of-war. Got that?"

"Yeah, Yeah, we got it," Spike replied, feigning disgust at Reggie's long-windedness.

As the other guys walked to their end of the battle field, Reggie barked out his final instructions, "Dan, you cover Wally. Mark, you take Pete. I'll handle Spike. Remember, guys, the only cover we have are.those small bushes and few scrubby trees. Don't waste your ammo. They're almost down there now. When I give the signal, get down there as fast as you can."

As the opposing team turned to face us, Reggie raised his right hand above his head for all to see. A moment later he dropped his hand to his side, signifying the battle had begun, and at the same time yelled, "Okay, guys, let's kick some butt!"

Defiant war-hoops erupted from both sides as we began running with abandonment toward each other.

I remember clearly the rush of adrenalin as I zeroed in on Pete. My heart was pounding uncontrollably as the gap between us narrowed.

At the moment our eyes made contact from about 100 feet, Pete knew I had singled him out. I couldn't believe the devious smile that greeted me, as if he were saying, "Come on and get me, if you got the guts."

At about 50 feet, and still on a dead-run, I let go my first salvo. *"Oh shit,"* I thought to myself, as my rubber band flew harmlessly over his left shoulder.

His response was immediate as he stopped abruptly, took aim and fired. His first shot was too close for comfort. I could hear its humming sound as the rubber band passed within an inch of my right ear.

Only 35 feet apart now, we both stood staring at each other, both feeling naked with empty guns in our hands. Almost simultaneously, we each dropped down behind the nearest thorn bush to reload.

As I worked feverishly to reload my weapon, I kept peeking out on the right side of the bush in order to monitor Pete's progress. Once I had loaded my gun, I decided to keep my concealment until Pete made the first move.

Peering through the edge of my bush, I finally saw Pete raise up slowly from behind his bush and begin walking stealthily toward me.

When he had approached to within a distance of 15 feet, I popped up and yelled, "Die!" as I fired point-blank at his chest. His mouth was agape with shock and his eyes saucer-sized, as the big, red rubber band found its mark and splatted loudly against his breast bone.

"O-O-O-W-W-W!" he howled, as he dropped his weapon and whipped up his shirt to survey the nasty red welt that was forming. "You'll pay for this, you son-of-a-bitch," he screamed, shaking his fist fiercely.

I couldn't stop chuckling as I ran off to reload again. I felt compelled to stop my retreat just long enough to yell back at Pete, "That's one, Big Guy. Remember, three and you're dead."

Once again reloading my gun behind the safety of a bush, I suddenly became aware of the commotion coming from the fence row bordering the pasture, at the top of hill. From 200 hundred feet away, I could see that Reggie, Spike, and Dan were very animated with excitement. Wally was no where to be seen.

Momentarily lost in thought, I had forgotten about Pete. All of a sudden, there he was in front of me, and I, still squatting, was looking directly into the business end of his rubber gun.

"Say your prayers, Asshole," he chortled, as he aimed the gun directly at my forehead.

"Wait a minute, Pete," I pleaded, trying to buy some time. "I gotta call time out."

"What the hell ya mean, time out?" he demanded angrily.

"Well somethin' bad is goin' on up on the hill. I think the other guys need us right away," I replied quickly.

Pete turned his attention to the frenzied activity at the top of hill. Turning back to me, he shook his head slowly, finally conceding, "Well, I guess you're right. We'd better get up there and see what's goin' on. But just remember, you're still my prisoner, and I just might decide to execute you later on."

As Pete and I approached the top of the hill, we began to understand what the panic was all about. Spike and Dan, who were leaning over the fence, appeared to be yelling frantically, while gesturing wildly toward the middle of the cow pasture. Reggie, who had actually crossed to the other side, stood at the edge of the pasture, screaming, "Stay right where ya are, Wally! We'll think of some way to getcha outta there!"

Pete and I were stunned to see the scene unfolding in amongst the cows, about 200 feet from the fence where we stood. There was Wally, clinging to the branches of a small tree, about eight feet above the ground. Beneath him, snorting and pawing at the ground, was a huge black bull. The red-eyed monster was so enraged that he would charge the trunk of tree head-on, causing it to shake violently under each impact.

Ashen-faced, Wally held on for dear life as the flimsy branches swayed wildly under each jolt of the huge black head. "C'mon, guys, ya gotta save me," he wailed plaintively. "This thing's tryin' ta kill me!"

"How the hell did this happen?" Pete asked; a question that was directed to no one in particular.

"Well, I guess it was my fault," Dan explained apologetically. "I had nailed 'im once in the ass, and then he took off up the hill. I guess he thought he could get away if he went in there with the cows. Who the hell knew that big bull was in there?"

By this time Reggie had joined us on our side of the fence. As we huddled around him, his face showed a seriousness that I'd never seen before. Pointing in the direction of Wally, he began to lay out the grim prospects of the situation. He narrowed his eyes as he spoke, "Look, guys, Wally can't hold on much longer with that big son-of-a-bitch batterin' the tree like that. And when he finally falls, he's gonna be dead meat. So we gotta do somethin' quick. Any suggestions?"

Spike was the first to speak. "Well, like my dad always says, "Desperate times call for desperate measures, and I think I got the desperate measure that just might work; that is, if I can sneak up behind that big, black mother."

"What the hell are you talkin' about, Spike?" Reggie demanded.

"Just hang loose, Compadre, and watch my smoke," Spike replied confidently, as he began to climb through the multi-stranded, barbed-wire fence. Once on the other side, with his trusty rubber gun held tightly in his right hand, he turned and said, "Besides, I owe him one."

"With a look of incredulity, Pete turned to me and said, "He ain't gonna take on that killer with just a rubber gun, is he?"

Totally without an answer, I could only shrug my shoulders.

Wally, who had become aware that Spike was moving in his direction, began to yell and wave his free arm frantically in an attempt to freeze the attention of the bull. It seemed to be working, as the bull charged the tree with even greater ferocity.

Slowly and stealthily Spike crept forward to align himself with the rear end of the black monster.

When Spike had progressed to within 15 feet of the bull's posterior, he raised his weapon slowly to fix his sights squarely on the target — those two massive black, hairy testicles that swayed ponderously between the bull's hind legs. The pendulous targets of choice hung suspended at least 16 inches below the animal's underside and were reminiscent of two gigantic egg plants that had somehow grown together.

Spike, cupping his left hand under the stock to steady his gun, released the projectile. Even from a distance of 200 feet, I could hear clearly the "Crack" as the knotted rubber band made hard contact with the fleshy mass of the bulbous appendages.

The four of us at the fence groaned in unison, as we imagined the bull's great pain at that instant.

The effect on the big, black creature was instantaneous. His high-pitched bellow seemed to move the leaves on the trees, as he rose stiff-legged three feet straight up.

Hitting the ground, the bull immediately swung his massive head to the rear to discover Spike feverishly trying to load another round. It was at that moment that the bull forgot all about Wally. He now had a new victim, and his rage had risen to volcanic proportions.

The bull seemed to spin his huge body 180 degrees through mid-air in order to position himself toward his adversary. Looking straight at Spike, who had now retreated to a spot 50 feet away, the black beast lowered his head, revealing an enormous pair of horns, which curved into menacing rapier-like points at the ends.

As the monster snorted ferociously and pawed at the ground, ready-ing himself for the charge, Spike decided then and there to end his career as a bull fighter. Dropping his rubber gun in blind panic, he turned and began a mad dash in our direction. The bull was in hot pur-suit and had closed to within a couple of feet when Spike reached our position and scurried under the bottom strand of the barbed wire.

The bull came skidding to a stop at the fence, directly in front of us. We could feel its hot breath and were frozen with fear as we stood face to face with the monster, only five strands of barbed wire separating us. We all breathed a sigh of relief when it finally turned away and began walking back to join the cows.

Well, needless to say, Wally was able to make it to safety during the time that Spike occupied the bull's attention.

None of us felt much like continuing the rubber-gun battle after that little diversion, so we packed up our guns and headed home.

On the return trip, Spike complained incessantly about the loss of his prized rubber gun. I chuckled to myself, thinking, *"Yeah, the rubber gun that now belonged to the big old bull with the high-pitched voice."*

That fall, a couple of months before his fifteenth birthday, Reggie began working part-time at a local bakery. His work schedule consisted of a few hours after school and all day on Saturday.

Spike and I were naturally envious of Reggie and his new found fortune; to think he actually got paid for working in such a neat place as Kneadem's Bakery. Where else could a fellow work that smelled so good and even allowed you to eat all the pastries you wanted?

The bakery environment was so intriguing that Spike and I began spending a lot of after-school time just hanging around, watching the baking processes and being entertained by the crazy antics of the work crew.

The crew at the bakery were, to say the least, an interesting lot; always pulling practical jokes on one another. They even had an initiation procedure for the new employees. One of the activities that befell the 'new guys' was to be sent to the basement Flour Room on an errand.

The Flour Room, dimly lit with a single incandescent bulb, was where several hundred 60-pounds bags of flour were stored. It was not a very clean place, with broken bags of flour everywhere and 6 to 8 inches of dirty sediment on the floor.

The most disgusting thing, however, was the severe infestation of giant cockroaches. These huge bugs swarmed everywhere, hundreds of them clinging from the ceiling. Many of them were albinos, the result of many generations of constant exposure to the white, powdery substance.

Large rats were also a common sight in this chamber of horrors.

The real initiation began a few moments after the new guy had entered the room and had had adequate time to view the 'creepy-crawlies'. Then, as he heard the door latch behind him, the light was switched off from outside the room, immersing the room in total blackness.

The whole gang would then gather outside the room and wait for the screams. Usually they had only to leave the new guy in the dark for a couple of minutes — long enough for a few of the crawly inhabitants to have climbed up his legs and taken residence on various body parts, or to have dropped from the ceiling on his head and neck. The brave ones — the new employees who successfully resisted the urge to scream — were treated to even a longer stay in the dark room.

Each new guy was also required to sniff the "German Sugar" that the Master Baker, Carl Helder, had brought with him from the old country, or so the story goes. The German Sugar was touted as being the sweetest smelling substance on the face of the earth, and was used on rare occasions by Mr. Helder to produce an exquisite German pastry.

The new guy was told that when the cap was taken off the quart jar, he would be allowed only one quick sniff. It was explained that prolonged exposure to air would reduce the potency of this priceless and irreplaceable ingredient. The new employee was encouraged to make his one sniff a substantial one, because he would never again have the privilege to partake of this most golden of fragrances.

Having been suitably primed, the victim could hardly wait to inhale the fragrance of this exotic German Sugar. With the entire crew assembled to watch the momentous event, one of the senior employees would produce the jar containing the white powder and remove the cap. Usually, with no need for further prompting, the new guy would rush forward eagerly to place his nose over the mouth of the jar.

After starting his deep breath, it was not uncommon for the new guy to abruptly stop inhaling, grab his throat, and start screaming in agony, while gasping for air. Other victims merely rolled their eyes back into their heads and collapsed in a heap — for the much anticipated "Fragrance of the Gods" turned out to be a substance known as powdered **ammonia**!

Carl Helder, the Chief Baker of the establishment, was a tall, gaunt man, with bushy eye brows and prominent black circles under his eyes. He reminded me very much of Boris Karloff, the guy who used to play the Frankenstein monster in the movies. His slow movement and thick German accent made him seem even more sinister.

Spike and I were always afraid to make eye-contact with Carl. I don't know what we thought would happen. For the most part, he seemed to ignore us; he seldom spoke to anyone. Even so, we always had this creepy feeling that he was watching us.

With all of his peculiarities, one in particular stood out: Carl never drank water — couldn't tolerate it. It made him nauseous. The only liquid he ever drank was beer. In fact, it was unusual to see the man ever eat anything. He kept his beer supply stored in the bakery's industrial-sized refrigerator, and probably drank over 24 bottles a day.

One day, his wife brought him a salad for his lunch. Apparently, there was some water either in the salad or in the dressing, because, after a few bites, Carl became nauseous and had to run to the restroom.

Some of the younger guys at the bakery would periodically pilfer one of Carl's beers; and then, so he wouldn't detect the missing beer right away, they would replace the missing contents with water and replace the bottle cap. It was just a matter of time until Carl selected that particular bottle. Of course, the results were all too predictable. Although the trick, if analyzed, seemed pretty mean-spirited, everyone had a big laugh when Carl rushed to the restroom, with his hand over his mouth.

It was not unusual to see Carl rushing to the restroom in this fashion. However, on one occasion the sequence was reversed. Reggie told about seeing Carl casually entering the restroom, with a girly magazine under his arm.

A few minutes later, a blood-chilling scream was heard emanating from the restroom, followed by a wild-eyed Carl bolting through the doorway, with his trousers still down around his ankles.

It took the astonished employees who surrounded him a long time to calm Carl down. Finally, in his broken English, he was able to explain his ordeal. It seems as though he was just sitting there on the stool, thoroughly enjoying his moment of sublimation, when a big rat came crashing through the ceiling and landed in his lap.

Having heard this hilariously human story, my impression of Carl softened a bit.

It became customary that, upon returning home from work, Reggie would bring with him a grocery sack full of freshly baked glazed donuts or an assortment of cookies. More often than not, I would wait up for him, so I could I gorge myself with goodies before going to bed.

One particular night, as Reggie and I sat eating some of the bakery's products in the family kitchen, Reggie related a story about a new guy they had just hired. The new guy, Joe something-or-other, had just reported for work that very night. After he was introduced to the other employees and given the standard, brief orientation, he was given his first task to perform. The night-shift supervisor took Joe to a small room next to the big ovens, and told him to open the wooden, 55-gallon, barrel of molasses that sat in middle of the room. Before he left, the supervisor informed Joe that he could find the proper tools in the cabinet against the wall.

Joe, anxious to please, assured the older man that he could handle the assignment and would have the barrel open in a jiffy. At this, the supervisor left the room.

Joe immediately went to the cabinet and selected his tool of choice: the biggest pry-bar he could find.

In less than 5 minutes, the supervisor returned to monitor Joe's progress. Immediately upon entering the room, he let go a string of obscenities. There was Joe, looking bewildered as he stood there ankle-deep in fresh molasses. The wooden barrel staves, which lay on the floor, were spread out in a circle, forming a near-perfect daisy design.

"What the hell did you do!" the supervisor demanded.

"All I did was open the barrel like ya told me to," Joe responded in a shaky voice.

"Yeah, ya dumb shit," the older guy screamed, "but I didn't tell ya to cut the metal bands that held the barrel together!" "Now get the scoop shovel, some mops, and hot water, and clean up this damn mess!"

Joe spent the next three hours cleaning up the molasses, during which time, each one of the older guys came around to laugh at him.

After the task was finally complete, Joe summoned the supervisor to observe the condition of the room, which now was cleaner than it had ever been and every drop of the sticky substance had been totally removed.

"Well, whadda ya think, Boss?" Joe said, beaming proudly.

"Well, I think ya did a pretty good job of cleaning up your mess, so I'm gonna give you the rest of the night off." the supervisor replied.

"No, shit!" Joe responded, smiling broadly.

"Yeah, in fact, you can have every night off from now on. You're fired! Pick up your final pay check Friday," the supervisor said matter-of-factly.

A stunned Joe left the bakery, never to return.

Reggie and some of the other guys thought he should have been given a second chance. The supervisor explained, however, that the seventy-five dollars it cost to replace the molasses was about two times the amount of Joe's weekly salary. He said the bakery just couldn't take a chance on a guy like that.

One night, about a week before Halloween, Spike and I went to a double-feature movie at the Harrison Theater.

We had an arrangement with Pete and Wally that, shortly after the first movie had begun, we would leave them in through the fire-exit door, which opened to the alley in back. We had done this many times for one another, without incident.

As I sat in the front row, munching on my popcorn and waiting for Spike to return with the other two guys, I chanced to look back toward the lobby. There, along side the last row of seats stood Mr. Jackson, the Theater Manager. Ol' Man Jackson was notorious for the way he harassed the younger patrons. He seemed to enjoy yelling at kids for making too much noise or having their feet on the seat in front of them.

At this moment, Mr. Jackson seemed to be staring intently toward the short corridor that ran along side the movie stage to the exit door — the same corridor that Spike had just used. It was as if this ill-tempered, old man suspected something. But there was no way to warn Spike and the other two guys, because they were already emerging from the corridor, through the red velvet drapes.

They never saw me making motions with my arms for them to go back out the exit door. By the time they reached the area where I sat, I could only blurt out, "We've been had, guys!" At that moment, Mr. Jackson, who was standing in the aisle, only a few feet behind me, said sternly, "Okay, Boys, come with me. We're gonna talk about this in my office."

He had already identified the four of us. So we had no choice but to fall in line in front of him, and walk up the long aisle past all the paying customers, who were laughing uproariously at our plight.

Being exposed to the public that way was very embarrassing. There was also a shared feeling of trepidation — not knowing what kind of punishment Mr. Jackson would mete out for such a dastardly act.

We all crowded into the small office on the basement level. Mr. Jackson sat behind the desk, staring at us with a dour expression. After a long pause, he spoke. "Well, boys, it seems we have a very serious matter here," he said in a low measured voice. "I should call the police and have you all hauled down to the jail," he continued. "Do you think that would be suitable punishment?"

The thought of the police being involved and all the consequences made my heart beat wildly.

Pete spoke up quickly, "Gee, Mr. Jackson, don't ya think that's pretty rough for a first offense?" "We're all real sorry for what we done, and I promise you, it'll never happen again," he said, showing as much remorse as he could muster. "Could ya please just let us go home, Mr. Jackson?" he pleaded.

Mr. Jackson, scowling, studied the four us for a long time. Finally, he said, "Well, I know I'll probably regret this, but I'm gonna give you kids a break."

Before he ejected us from the theater, he delivered a stern warning that we'd better never engage again in such corrupt behavior. He also told us that we'd be banned from the theater for one month.

Everyone, except Spike, felt that we had gotten off pretty easy.

Outside the theater, Spike began to carp about how unfair the whole thing was.

"How the hell do you figger we got treated unfairly, Spike?" Pete asked pointedly. "All he did was scold us and then told us we couldn't come back for a month. If my 'ol man had found out about this, I'd be in deep shit."

"Well, it was the way he humiliated us by paradin' us up that aisle, past everybody," Spike fumed. " "Geez, I saw Mary Alice Stempel sittin' there with her family. You guys know I kinda like her. Now I'll never be able to look her in the eye again. You can be sure of one thing, though, I'm gonna get even with that ol' fart," Spike vowed.

"Hey, you guys wanna go over to the bakery with me and wait for Reg to get off work?" I asked.

"I'll go with ya," Spike replied.

"I would, but I gotta get home by 9:30," Pete responded.

"I think I'll head home, too," Wally added. "C'mon, Pete, I'll walk ya part way."

Spike and I walked across Main Street toward the bakery, while Pete and Wally headed up the hill, toward home.

We entered the side door, which opened into the Packaging Room, where all the wrapping machinery was set up. All the bakery personnel were loafing around in the Packaging Room, taking their break.

Reggie, who had been talking to two other employees, spotted us as we stepped inside. "Hey, guys, over here," he yelled.

We walked around the big bread-wrapping machine and each of us took a seat on the wooden table, on either side of Reggie.

"I thought you guys were gonna take in the double feature tonight. Was the first movie so bad that ya had to leave early?" Reggie asked.

"Not exactly, Reg," Spike replied, and then went on to relate the whole sordid story.

We must have touched Reggie with our sad story, because he bought each of us a coke from the employees pop machine.

Spike and I sat drinking our cokes and talking to Reggie for 5 minutes or so, when Reggie said, "Well, fellas, I gotta get back to work. If ya wanna wait around 'til 9:30, I'll walk home with ya."

"Okay, we'll just hang around and watch you poor suckers work," I replied, smiling.

"Just don't get in the way," Reggie cautioned, as he headed back to the corner of big processing room, where the glazed donuts were about to be produced.

Spike and I walked back to the loading area, where the big overhead doors opened to the alley. A large number of pressed-paper barrels full of baked goods sat there, awaiting the morning trash pickup.

"Man, look at all this stuff they're throwin' out," Spike commented. "It'd sure feed a lot of hungry people."

"Yeah, but Reg says they gotta throw the stuff out when it reaches the expiration date printed on each package," I explained. "Ya know, most of this stuff has been returned from the grocery stores. I guess some farmer will pick it up to feed to his pigs."

"What a waste," Spike replied, shaking his head.

Spike's gaze suddenly fixed on a spot beyond the stack of barrels. Peering over the last row of barrels, he yelled, "Hey, look over here, Mark, an egg crate half fulla' eggs!" "Whydya think they're throwin' these out?" he asked.

"I guess they're spoiled," I replied.

"Well, if they're rotten, nobody needs 'em anymore," he mused.

"Just what the hell are you gettin' at?" I demanded.

"I just thought of a great way to get even with ol' man Jackson," he said, grinning wickedly.

"I don't think I'm gonna like this," I responded warily.

"Just listen to my plan," Spike urged. "I think you'll like it. Ya see, all we do is take these eggs down the alley to the back of Richie's Restaurant. Then we just heave 'em over the restaurant as hard as we can." "You know what's right across Main Street from Richie's, don't ya?" he asked, his eyes gleaming brightly."

"You wanna egg the front of the Harrison Theater, right? Are you crazy, Spike?" I asked, my voice cracking.

"Hell, yeah!" he shouted back. "We can do the deed and be gone before anyone knows who done it." "Are ya with me, or not?" he demanded.

"Yeah, I guess so," I replied reluctantly. "But let's make our getaway through that passageway that runs between the music store and Pete's Chili Parlor."

"Good idea, Mark. That way, we'll come back out on Main Street, and be able to see the damage first-hand," Spike replied enthusiastically.

We left the bakery through the rear door, which was located next to the overhead door installation.

I had a nervous feeling in my stomach as we carried the half-full egg crate down the dimly lit alley. We passed by the escape passageway on our way to our destination, which was only a half-block away.

Finally, we turned into the small parking area that ran behind Richie's, and sat our burden down in the gravel. Since Richie's had closed earlier in the evening, this area was bathed in darkness. I felt a little more secure after seeing how dark our launch area actually was.

From where we stood, we could look over Richie's one-story structure and see clearly the brightly lit upper two stories of the three-story theater. The bottom story and marquee were hidden from view.

"Well, let's get to it," Spike whispered matter-of-factly.

At that moment, we each started grabbing eggs, one in each hand, and began to furiously lob them over the restaurant. Almost at once, we heard screaming.

"Oh, my God!" I thought to myself. *"The movie is just leaving out, and we're bombarding the customers."*

"C'mon, Mark, fire 'em faster!" Spike whispered frantically. "We can't stay here much longer!"

We had almost emptied the crate, when we heard the siren. A police car was heading in our direction.

"Oh, shit, we better shag ass!" Spike screamed.

We could already see the squad car entering the north end of the alley.

Spike, who was running fast, a few feet ahead of me, abruptly made his cut to the right. What he thought was the opening to the passageway was only the shadow of a telephone pole being cast on the bricks by the lone light that illuminated the alley.

All I heard was "O-O-O-mph!" as Spike bounced off the brick wall, and landed on his butt on the wet, cobble-stone surface. Seeing that he was in a dazed condition, I grabbed him under the arms and half-dragged him to the entrance of the passageway, a few feet away.

We had just concealed ourselves in a dark corner beneath a fire escape, when the squad car, lights flashing, came screaming down the alley and right on by the passageway entrance.

"C'mon, Spike, let's get out on Main Street before the cops come back here," I said, as I helped him to his feet.

Spike, having quickly gained his senses, was able to walk to the Main Street end of the passageway without assistance.

"Geez, will ya look at that," Spike said, as we stepped out on the Main Street sidewalk, and looked in the direction of the Harrison Theater. "C'mon, let's walk across the street and mingle with the crowd. Nobody'll notice us that way," he added.

A crowd had gathered out front of the theater. Everyone was milling around, looking up and pointing, and talking about the egg bombardment. Eggs were running down the front of the building and dripping off the edge of the marquee. Eggs had smashed against the glass-enclosed box office, and people were slipping on the eggs that covered the sidewalk.

In the middle of this chaos stood Mr. Jackson, wiping egg yoke from his glasses. The three yellow blotches on his suit coat were evidence that he'd caught more than one of the "incoming."

To my shock, Spike walked right up to Mr. Jackson. "Gee, what happened here, Mr. Jackson?" he asked all innocent-like.

"Well, I'm not sure exactly," was Mr. Jackson's response. "I had just opened the front doors to let the early-movie crowd out, when all hell broke loose," he said, shaking his head, as he wiped his glasses vigorously with his handkerchief. "All at once, eggs came rainin' down on everyone. I had to run for cover to keep from gettin' totally covered with these damn things. I don't know how I'll ever get this stuff off my suit," he complained bitterly.

"Gosh, that's too bad, Mr. Jackson," Spike said, feigning compassion. "Them eggs musta been purty ripe, 'cause you don't smell so good, either. I sure hope you're able to get whoever done this to you."

"Oh, we'll get 'em, alright. Don't you worry. And when we get 'em, they're gonna pay," he said, scowling.

"Well, be seein' ya, Mr. Jackson," Spike said in a friendly fashion, as he turned away to join me at the back of the crowd.

As Spike walked toward me, I could hear ol' man Jackson calling after him, "Don't forget, you boys aren't allowed back in here for a month!"

"Blow it out your ass, ol' man," Spike said under his breath.

"C'mon, let's get back to the bakery," I suggested. "It's about time for Reg to be gettin' off."

"Yeah, I guess we did enough for one night," Spike said, smiling, while nudging me with his elbow.

On the way home that night, we told Reggie the whole story.

His reaction surprised us. We anticipated that he'd think the whole escapade was pretty neat — something he might have thought of himself. Instead, he scolded us for having done such a stupid thing, and said we must have been out of our minds to pull a stunt like that. He admonished us further by saying, "All I can say is, you guys acted pretty damn childish tonight."

I guess he was right, but something bothered me. I realized then that Reggie was beginning to sound like the rest of the grownups. Did this mean he wouldn't be doing kid stuff with us anymore?

That night in bed I felt sad and lonely — almost as if I'd lost a brother.

It became gradually apparent that Reggie was indeed growing up. His job responsibilities and exposure to the older bakery employees — some married with children — had definitely made him more worldly and serious-minded.

Except for the brief sledding adventure the two of us would share during the forthcoming Christmas vacation, nearly two years would pass before Reggie and I would begin sharing good times on a regular basis. Our closeness was destined to resume in the fall of 1947, around the time that Reggie purchased his first car and began inviting me and some of the other guys along for some cruisin' up and down Main Street.

For now, though, the other guys and I would just have to find our own fun, and survive without Reggie's leadership.

Although it was traditional for 'trick-or-treating' to be carried out the entire month of October, Spike, Pete, Wally, and I held off until the last week of October to pull our Halloween capers.

On Friday night, two days before Halloween, we decided to try our luck in the Heather Heights area, which was located in the northwest corner of the city.

Heather Heights was recognized as the most affluent neighborhood in the city of Harrington. The most prominent families resided there in their palatial magnificence.

Ordinarily, the likes of us would not be seen in this area. But at Halloween time, what teenager could resist the best pickin's in town? The Heather Heights residents were usually good for cake, cookies, high-quality chocolate candy, or silver coins — no homemade popcorn balls and apples here.

However, some of the more snobbish members of this exclusive neighborhood were quick to let us know that we were not welcome in their part of town. This usually amounted to having the door slammed in our faces after we delivered our "Trick or Treat" greeting. It was these residents that we saved our special tricks for.

Of course, we used some of the more conventional tricks on some of the lesser offenders. These pranks included: ringing a doorbell repeatedly, and then running away before the occupant could open the door; soaping windows; shoving foreign matter through the door's mail slot; and "setting horns" on the cars parked curbside.

The setting of car horns required two things: an unlocked car and a two-foot section cut from a limber tree branch. While someone watched the front door to warn if the car owner appeared, one of the guys would get inside the car and weave the tree branch under the outer ring on one side of the steering wheel, up and over the horn device in the center hub, and then under the outer ring on the opposite side of the steering wheel; thus locking down the horn actuator so that the horn would blare incessantly until the owner could get there to remove the stick that was pushing down on the horn.

Usually, we would wait in some natural concealment to watch the owner's reaction to the blaring horn. It would sometimes take a long time for the person to realize that it was his car making the offensive noise. Then, he would race outside — often time in his pajamas and bare feet — to try and put an end to the infernal racket. Of course, most of the time loud obscenities accompanied the owner's trip to the great outdoors.

So far this night we had spent several hours conducting our Trick-or-Treat tour through this well-to-do neighborhood. In the process, we had collected an abundance of goodies, which we ate along the way. Conversely, the non-compliant residents were treated to one of our tricks. To this juncture, we had had occasion to use every one of our more common tricks at least once. However, we had not yet subjected anyone to the dreaded "Hot Shit" prank.

There was a strikingly pretty, blond-haired girl living in the Heather Heights neighborhood, whom I admired very much. Cindy Logan was in my class at St. Matthew's, and for many years I was taken by her stunning looks and above-average intelligence. Of course, she never knew I existed, nor did I give her any reason to think I had a crush on her.

Anyway, since I was in her neighborhood this particular night, I felt compelled to try something at Cindy's house, where she resided with her mother and two older sisters — both school teachers in the public school system. Cindy's father, who had been a wealthy industrialist in the city, had died a few years earlier.

I walked to front door of Cindy's house, as the other guys waited for me in the darkened alley, across the street. I stood on the front porch, wondering what to do next, when I noticed the big mail slot in the front door. I Immediately crouched down at eye-level to the mail slot and pushed the spring-loaded flap in.

I discovered that by peering into the mail-slot opening, I could survey the entire foyer area of the big house and could see anyone entering the foyer from the main part of the house and would therefore be alerted to anyone starting down the 20-foot hallway toward the front door. This arrangement gave me the perfect opportunity to ring the doorbell and be able to run the instant I saw someone coming my way.

This scheme worked to perfection. I could actually reach the doorbell on the right side of the doorway, while in the crouched position, peering through the slot. In this fashion, I would give the doorbell button several fast bursts, and within seconds, I would see one of Cindy's older sisters entering the foyer from the big living room. I would immediately turn and run across the street to meet the other guys in the alleyway.

From the shadows of the alley, we observed one of the older Logan sisters open the front door, step outside, and look up and down the street. Then, with a disgusted look on her face, she spun around and walked back inside, slamming the door behind. Back in the alley, we thought this was great fun, watching the frustration grow as the sisters came to the door time after time, until after the fifth time, the one sister cursed loudly, as she stood there with her hands on her hips, looking up and down the street.

As we stood in the alley, Spike commented, "Mark, that shit's gettin' purty old. Maybe ya oughta find somethin' else to do to 'em." "Hey, look," he said, pointing in the direction of Cindy's house, "now they're all lookin' out the windows, tryin' to see who's been causin' all the trouble."

At that moment, I was blessed with a great new idea, which I immediately shared with other guys.

"Listen to this, guys," I said excitedly. "When I was lookin' through the mail slot, I noticed that their telephone is sittin' on a little stand right inside the front door, on the right side. I think I can get my arm far enough inside to reach the phone." "You know what happens when ya leave the phone off the hook?" I asked.

Pete was the first to answer, "Sure, after the phone's off the hook for a while, it starts beepin', so what?"

"Well, don't ya think that would drive 'em nuts after a while?" I asked impatiently.

"It sure would sure piss me off," Wally admitted.

"Well, then, I'm gonna do it," I said resolutely. "But first, I gotta wait 'til things cool down — 'til they're all away from the windows."

In about 10 minutes, everything seemed to be back to normal, so I walked slowly back to the front door. The other guys waited in the alley.

Crouching in front of the door, I peeked through the mail slot to make certain no one was waiting in the foyer. Glancing to the right, I could see the telephone about two feet away. The only way that I could reach it was to raise my head above the slot level, and thrust my entire right arm inside. I became immediately aware that in this position, I had lost my advantage to be able to detect someone heading in my direction.

"Oh, well," I thought to myself, *"I've come this far." "If I don't go through with it now, the guys will think I'm chicken."*

With my arm pushed inside to where my shoulder blocked any further extension, I groped to the right side for the feel of the telephone. I finally made contact with my fingertips, and, with some effort, was able to lift the receiver up and lay it on the surface of the table.

Having accomplished this, I withdrew my arm from the slot and stood beside the door, waiting for the phone to begin beeping. As soon as the phone started making its obnoxious beeping sound, I left the porch and ran around to the corner of the house, where I could monitor the front door from concealment, but still be seen by the guys in the alley.

From my vantage point, I waved to the guys, letting them know I had accomplished my mission.

As I peered around the corner of the house, I could still the hear the incessant beeping sound. Suddenly, the sound ceased. A moment later, the front door flew open, and one of Logan sisters stepped out on the porch, angrily casting her gaze around the front of the house. A few moments later, she stomped back into the house.

I waited a full five minutes before repeating the process. I was again able to remove the telephone and return to my hiding place without being detected.

On my third try, I began the procedure as always, by peering through the mail slot. Confirming that the hallway was clear, I reached my arm in and felt for the phone. It didn't seem to be in the same place. As I groped around without success, a question came to mind: "Could some have moved the phone?" I had a terrible sense of foreboding and started to pull my arm back out, when suddenly, something or someone grabbed my wrist and held tight, causing my heart to almost leap from my chest.

As I pulled with all my might to free myself, I could hear one of the sisters say, "Now, that we got the little bastard, we'll fix him good. Here, help me hold him while I cut one of his goddamn fingers off!"

Completely terrified by now, I let out a scream, "Holy Shit, they're gonna cut my fingers off." "Help!

Spike was the first to arrive. Standing behind me, with his arms around my waste, he began pulling me away from the door. Pete and Wally, in turn, fell in behind and tugged on Spike to add more power to this life and death struggle.

I had become the "rope" in this mortal tug-of-war!

Just as it seemed we were making progress in our direction, I felt a searing pain on the back of my right hand. "Oh, my, God, they already started cuttin' on me!" I screamed in horror.

The surge of adrenalin from my team gave us the momentary advantage we needed. My hand came free from the unseen death-grip, causing the four of us to fall backward into a heap on the front porch.

As we scurried round on the porch floor, trying to regain our feet, we could hear the sisters laughing hysterically behind the door, and one them saying, "Well, I don't think that little son-of-a -bitch will be bothering us anymore tonight."

The four of us made a mad scramble down the steps and through the front yard, falling over one another in our attempt to reach the safety of the alley. We ran two blocks down the darkened alleyway before we stopped under a street light.

I had been holding my left hand tightly over the back of my right hand, afraid to view the knife wound.

"Here, let me look at that," Spike said, pulling my left hand away. "Hell, you didn't get cut with no knife. Them crazy bitches put a cigarette out on the back of your hand," he chortled.

Sure enough, there was the tell-tale black smudge surrounding a reddened area, and a sizeable blister was rising in the center.

"Hell, I really thought they were gonna cut me," I said, now laughing as much from nervous relief as from the humor of the moment.

"Ya know somethin', fellas," Wally said, looking very serious, "I never knew them teachers knew cuss words like that."

We laughed so hard that we were too weak to stand any longer, and were forced to sit on the curb until the infectious uproar subsided.

After the laughter died down, Pete rose from his sitting position and said, "It's after 9:00, fellas. I'd better be headin' home."

"Not yet, Pete," Spike pleaded. "We ain't pulled the "Hot Shit" trick yet. Ya know, Ol' Man Jackson from the theater lives just a block down the street. C'mon, guys, let's go back in the alley and fill this up, he said, pulling a paper bag from his jacket pocket."

"Well, okay, I guess," Pete finally conceded. "But it better not take too long, and we better damn sure not get caught."

"No sweat," Spike replied reassuringly.

Having led the way to a very dark spot behind a garage, Spike held the bag out and whispered, "I hope somebody can muster up a crap."

"Here, give it to me, Spike," Wally responded. "I been havin' ta go for about an hour. We had soup beans for supper, so it's gonna stink real bad," he warned, So you guys better stand back."

"Yeah, but can ya fill it up?" Pete asked.

"No problem," Wally answered, as he headed into the deep shadows with the empty paper sack.

The rest of us went to the alley and waited.

After a few minutes, Wally came sauntering out with the sack in his hand. "Here, Spike," he said, shoving the sack under Spike's nose.

Repulsed by the overwhelming odor, Spike recoiled, screaming, "Goddamit, Wally, get that smelly thing outta here!" With his right hand cupped over his nose, he continued his tirade. "My Gawd, Wally, did somethin' crawl up in ya and die? Close that damn sack up, will ya, before ya make us all sick."

With Wally carrying our "secret weapon," we headed out in the direction of Mr. Jackson's house.

As Pete and I waited behind some bushes, in a vacant lot across the street, Spike and Wally crept up the steps to Mr. Jackson's front porch.

Once on the porch, Wally partially opened the sack and sat it on the floor.

Spike with his book of matches already out, struck a match and held it to upper edges of the paper sack. Shortly the top of the sack burst into flames.

Wally immediately began ringing Mr. Jackson's door bell, while using the small window in the door to monitor the inside.

As soon as he caught sight of Mr. Jackson, in his robe and house slippers, ambling toward the front door, He yelled to spike, "Let's get the hell outta here!"

Spike and Wally had just joined Pete and I, behind the bushes, when the front door flew open.

"What the hell!" Mr. Jackson yelled, as he began stomping out the fire.

Of course, as he stomped, the human excrement flew. By the time he realized what he had stepped into, the brown stinky matter covered his house slippers and even sprayed up his pajama legs.

"Oh, my God!" he screamed, as the sight and odor assaulted his senses.

At that moment, his wife leaned out the door, and said, "What's all the commotion about, Henry?"

"Someone just tricked me into stompin' on a bag full shit. That's all," he said angrily.

"Well, you go out back and hose yourself off right now," she ordered. "You're not gettin' back in the house smellin' like that."

On his way to the back of the house, Mr. Jackson stopped momentarily at the bottom of his front steps and seemed to stare in our direction. Shaking his fist in the air, he yelled "I know you little bastards are out there somewhere, and I'm gonna find out who you are and make you pay dearly!"

Somehow we managed to sneak into the alley without Ol' Man Jackson hearing our muffled laughter.

Just as we were about to head east down the alley, in the direction of our homes, Spike jumped out in front and turned facing the rest of us. "Wait a minute, fellas!" he said excitedly. "We got time for one more thing. Hell, this may be the last chance we'll ever get do this together again. What say, we let it all hang out?"

"Man, count me out," Pete responded, sounding a little agitated. "It's almost 10. I'm headin' home."

As Pete walked quickly away from us, Spike let go loudly with his famous chicken call, "Br-r-o-ock, br-r-o-o-ck, br-r-o-o-ck!"

Without looking back, Pete, who had progressed about 50 feet, merely raised his right hand in a "one-finger" salute and continued walking easterly.

"Chicken-shit," Spike said, feigning contempt, not loud enough for Pete to hear.

"Okay, what's the deal, Spike?" I inquired impatiently. "I can't stay out too much later."

"Well, if you and Wally got the balls, I'll take you on a tour of the cemetery over by Memorial Park," Spike responded with a devious grin.

"Lead the way, Big Man," I said in a goading fashion, while hoping he would change his mind.

"Yeah, count me in, too." Wally added, the cracking of his voice betraying his apprehension.

It took less than ten minutes to cover the eight blocks that brought us to the main gate of the Mount Hope Cemetery.

For some reason, we paused momentarily before going through the gate. I guess the environment didn't appear as inviting as we had imagined. We stood there at the bottom of the hill, not speaking, just surveying all the headstones and monuments on the hillside. All eyes focused finally on the largest structure in the cemetery. The huge, gray limestone mausoleum, with its ornate Roman pillars, loomed high above the surrounding landscape.

There at the top of the hill, the mausoleum stood out eerily, lit dimly by the full moon, which peeked in and out from behind the moving storm clouds. Broken patches of ground fog enshrouded the base of the building, giving it the appearance of floating on a layer of clouds.

Although the temperature hovered around the mid-forties, I suddenly felt chilled to the bone.

Without a word being said, we started walking slowly up the main driveway toward the gray-stone mausoleum. It was almost as if some magnetic force were drawing us toward this foreboding structure. As we drew near the structure, I could feel the palms of my hands begin to sweat.

Wally and I paused at the bottom of the dozen or so steps that led up to the two enormous, ornamental metal doors that provided entry into the inner sanctum of the mausoleum. Without hesitation, Spike bounded up the steps and, grabbing the door handle on the right side, turned and yelled at us, "C'mon, dammit! We ain't got all day."

A moment later, Wally and I were on the landing with Spike, helping him pull open the heavy door. "Cr-r-r-eak," the heavy door groaned in protest, as we slowly gained some advantage over its weight. When the door was opened sufficiently, Spike stepped inside, followed by me, then Wally. The sudden darkness that met us made it difficult to even see one another. The fetid smell of long-dead flowers assaulted our nostrils.

Standing inside the vestibule, we strained to see into the void of the dark, dank main chamber that lie just ahead, beyond the huge archway, which resembled a pair of ghostly arms waiting to enfold us.

We slowly shuffled forward, staying as closely packed as possible. For some reason, we only spoke in whispers, maybe out of respect for the dead, but most probably, it was the apprehension that began to overwhelm us.

Once inside the main chamber, one could distinguish a small porthole-like window mounted high on the 15-foot wall at each end of the long corridor. The moonlight captured by the two small windows was barely sufficient to cast a dim glow at the ceiling level; however, periodic flashes of lightning provided additional bursts of illumination.

As our eyes became more acclimated to the darkness, we could perceive vaguely the square configurations along the far wall. We all knew that these squares, which bore inscriptions identifying the interred person, were the result of the concrete seals that completed each entombment. Each vertical row accommodated four tombs. Some were filled and sealed off; others were just square, horizontal holes, awaiting a future occupant.

How it happened, I'm not sure. But I found myself leading the other two in a right-hand direction along the wall. Spike was grasping my left hand tightly as I slid my right hand along the cold, damp vertical surface ahead of me. I assumed that Wally was holding onto Spike's left hand.

Halfway down the wall, I felt something that filled me with panic. I let go a gasp as my hand suddenly dropped into an opening that was not empty.

It took me a moment to catch my breath and to realize that what I was holding on to, a foot or so inside the horizontal hole, was the type of large metal handle that adorned the end of a casket. My arm jerked back in revulsion.

Spike, sensing my fright, whispered nervously, "What the hell happened, Mark?"

My voice was still shaky, when I pulled him close and said, "T-t-t-here's a casket in there. I think they had a burial service today, and they haven't sealed off the tomb yet."

"No shit!" he responded, in a high-pitched whisper. "C'mon, let's keep movin'." I could then hear Spike whispering an explanation to a worried Wally.

Another shock was awaiting us in the deep, dark recesses at the end of the corridor. As we neared the end of the entombment wall, I heard something that made the hair rise on the nape of my neck. *"My God, that's someone breathing!"* I thought, as my heart tried to leap from my chest cavity.

By now, I was too close to whatever or whomever it was to react rationally. All I could do is scream, "Run for your lives! There's someone back here!"

With the adrenalin pumping furiously, I turned to run. *"Holy, shit! Somethin's gotta hold of my pants leg. I'm a goner now!"*

As I tugged to free myself, the rush of blood pounding in my temples nearly drowned out the sound of the two pairs of running footsteps that were becoming fainter as they echoed down the long corridor.

Realizing now that I was being abandoned, I screamed out desperately, "Help me, guys! Somethin's gotta hold a me!"

The footsteps only picked up momentum. I knew all was lost when I heard the big metal door clang shut. I was now alone with whatever was holding me captive.

Although my left pant leg was being held tightly, I made one last furious attempt to free myself. With extreme effort, I kicked back with my right heel, making hard contact with the heap that was my captor. A loud groan emanated from behind me, and my leg was instantly released. I did not look back as I ran down the corridor.

Finally reaching the big doors, I began tugging desperately to open them. I could hear a shuffling noise moving down the corridor in my direction. I had visions of a monster, much like the one I had seen in the movie "The Mummy's Tomb," with rotting strips of cloth hanging from its body and dragging one foot as it progressed inexorably toward me. I could not seem to budge the heavy door.

At the moment the shuffling sound seemed almost upon me, the door sprung open. Spike and Wally had finally come to my aid and were pulling from the other side. At the first opportunity, I jumped through the small opening and into the cool night air, feeling ecstatic that I had escaped the clutches of a terrible fate. My exhilaration was short-lived, however, as I began to realize that the creature would soon be at the door. Waves of panic again rolled over me.

"What the hell happened in there?" Spike demanded nervously.

"Somethin' had a hold a me, and it's still in there," I responded almost hysterically. "If we're gonna make it outta here alive, we'd better get our asses movin'!"

"Bullshit, Mark! Now just settle down," Spike replied, hoping to calm me. "You're just lettin' your imagination get the best of you."

I must have looked totally bewildered as I stared at Spike, searching for a way to make him take me more seriously, when, suddenly, the big door began to slowly creak open. At that moment, the three of us could only stand there at the bottom of the steps, too frozen with fear to move. It was too late to run.

I'm sure our eyes were popping from their sockets and mouths were agape as we fixed our gaze on the ever greater opening. We gasped in unison as the figure moved from the darkness into our vision.

There in front of us, at the top of the steps, stood this old wino, the tell-tale, brown-paper sack still gripped tightly in his hand. He obviously had been sleeping one off in the mausoleum.

He stood there on unsteady legs, surveying us sternly. "What the hell are you boys up to?" he demanded. "Hell, a man can't even find a place to sleep anymore. Now get the hell outta here before I do somethin' bad to ya," he said as menacingly as possible.

Spike began laughing hysterically, causing Wally and me to break into uncontrolled laughter also. Along the way home, we kept erupting into laughter just reviewing the events of the evening.

However, at one point in the journey home that night, everyone turned unexplainably quiet. It was then that Wally shared an observation with Spike and I: "Ya know, fellas, this Halloween stuff's not as much fun as it used to be." Ironically, I had been thinking the same thing, which prompted me to reply, "I hafta agree, Wally. Maybe we're gettin' too old to enjoy pullin' those tricks anymore."

"Yeah, I guess we oughta leave that stuff to the kids from now on," Spike said dejectedly, with his head bowed.

Maybe it was just a sign of growing up, but we all seemed to agree that night that Halloween pranks had lost their appeal. Nevertheless, I think we all felt a sense of sadness knowing that we would never again participate in this kind of Halloween frivolity.

Adjusting to my first semester as a Freshman at Harrington Catholic High School was a little tougher than I had anticipated. So when Christmas vacation rolled around, it was most welcome. It meant almost two weeks free from the rigors of high school life.

The Gearing family enjoyed an excellent Christmas season. Dad had gotten a substantial raise from the dairy and was able to purchase more and better presents than in times past. In addition, Reggie, who had a steady income from his job at the bakery, bought gifts for all the family members.

Even the weather cooperated. It snowed Christmas eve and all day Christmas. An accumulation of about 8 inches of fresh snow made the whole Harrington area glisten with wintry beauty.

The day after Christmas offered perfect conditions for sledding — bright and clear, with a temperature in the teens, and plenty of snow.

The guys met at my house around 9:00 that morning. For a while, we all sat in the living room discussing the Christmas gifts we had each received. Everyone seemed pretty satisfied with their presents, even though we had all received more clothing than anything else.

After I had bid Mom good-bye, the four of us went outside to pick up our sleds. My old five-foot sled was seeing its third winter, but was still in good shape. Wally had an older one, also. Spike had just received a new sled for Christmas, and he was anxious to try it out.

Pete surprised us all. He showed up with a brand new sliding device — a strange looking, all-wood contraption, whose front end curved back in the shape of a hook. None of us had ever seen anything like it.

Spike, on the verge of laughing, asked, "Whadda ya call that goofy lookin' thing, Pete?"

"That's the toboggan my mom and dad got me for Christmas, and don't make fun of it!" Pete shot back angrily. "It'll sure as hell beat anything here on good snow, and it'll carry four people."

"Well, 'seein's believin'," Spike said tauntingly. "Let's take it over to the hill at Harrington Labs and try it out."

It took less than 5 minutes to reach the top of the big hill that ran down the west side of the Harrington Labs property. The incline was fairly steep and ran downhill for about 700 feet, before leveling off and running another 150 feet to Lipton Street.

"Well, climb on, guys," Pete said, as he sat in the front of the toboggan, with his feet up inside the curved portion. "We'll give this baby its maiden voyage."

As we sat there with the toboggan pointed down the hill, Pete explained how we would master this strange craft.

"First of all, this doesn't operate like a sled," he began. "We all hafta lean in the direction we wanna turn. I'll yell out orders when it's time ta lean and in what direction." Continuing his instructions, he said, "Spike, since you're in the back, you'll hafta give us a good push and then jump in after we get goin' good. Any questions?"

"Yeah," Spike replied, as he crawled out of the toboggan. "Is it okay to start pushin' now, Professor?" he asked sarcastically"

Pete, ignoring the sarcasm, just raised his right hand and pushed it forward, signaling Spike to begin his push.

With his hands on Wally's shoulders, Spike began pushing us over the crest of the hill. After about 30 feet, we had picked up sufficient speed, and Spike jumped on board and pulled his feet inside for the big ride.

It wasn't long before we were 'swooshing' down the hill at a good rate, with Pete yelling commands: "Lean right, lean left!" We were soon good enough as a team to dodge the lone tree near the bottom of hill. The feeling of speed and the ability to turn the craft instantly was much like the exhilaration I imagined a downhill skier would feel on a good course.

As we got out of the toboggan at the bottom of the hill, only about 50 feet from the Lipton Street curb, it was obvious Spike had been converted when he said, "I gotta admit, Pete, that sure beats the hell out of a sled ride. Let's get up there and do it again."

"Okay," Pete replied. "But let's be sure to keep goin' down the same course. It'll get even better when the snow gets packed down good. One thing's for sure, we don't want no sleds on our toboggan slide. Those metal runners will really tear up the surface."

"You don't hafta worry about sleds no more," Wally said reassuringly. "I think everybody would rather keep ridin' the toboggan."

After sliding down the hill for an hour or so, someone came up with the bright idea of building a ramp so we could "ski-jump" with the toboggan. At first, Pete argued that that kind of treatment would surely damage his toboggan. But he finally relented under pressure and the assurance we wouldn't build a very high ramp and that only one guy at a time would take the toboggan over the jump.

For the foundation of the ramp, we borrowed some cardboard boxes of beeswax that were stacked behind the Labs' main building. We began constructing our ramp at a point about 200 feet down the incline. We stacked the 50-pound boxes in a stair-step fashion. The structure was four boxes wide, and the first row (farthest forward) was four boxes high; the second row was three high; the third row, two high; and fourth row (the start of the ramp) was one box high.

While Pete and Wally continued stacking the boxes, Spike went back to my house with me to pick up a 4- by 8-foot sheet of plywood that my dad had stored in the garage.

As Spike and I struggled to carry the plywood back to the toboggan course, we were met by two guys from the neighborhood who had been sliding on some of the hilly streets around the area.

"Hey, what you guys doin'?" Charlie Walton inquired.

Spike and I put our load down to rest for a moment and contemplated how to answer the question.

I figured we could use the help, and the two Walton brothers, Charlie and Bob, were okay guys, so I finally replied, "Well, Charlie, I'll let ya in on a secret, if you'll help us carry this plywood over to the Labs."

"Sure, Bob and me will help ya," Charlie said, his eyes wide with excitement. "Just cut us in on the secret."

"Well, Guys," I explained, "we got us a good slidin' place over on the hill next to the Harrington Labs, and we're gonna use this plywood to finish our ski-jump ramp. Only it ain't gonna be a ski-jump exactly. We're gonna take Pete Rocelli's toboggan over the jump."

"What's a toboggan?" Bob asked, with a blank look.

"You'll see soon enough," Spike answered. "Now let's get this plywood movin'," he said, his impatience beginning to wear thin.

"Okay," Charlie responded. "But we don't really hafta carry the plywood, ya know. Just lay it on top of our sleds, and we can just pull it."

"That's a good idea," I thought to myself. *"Why didn't Spike and I bring our own sleds?"*

As we walked toward the Labs, I explained to Charlie and Bob that they couldn't use their sleds on the same course that was being used for the toboggan slide. They understood the damage that could be done to the toboggan course and accepted the fact that another part of the hill could be used for sleds.

Pete didn't seem too happy that Spike and I showed up with two more guys; but he didn't press the issue, because he knew the Walton brothers would help us finish our project more quickly.

The six of us began working furiously to finish the ramp. We packed snow in the "steps" made by the rows of boxes and smoothed the snow to form as perfect a ramp shape as we could. We then laid the plywood over the ramp structure. To finish the process, we packed several inches of snow on top of the plywood, and smoothed the snow out by running the empty toboggan back-and-forth over the surface. When we completed the job, the ramp surface had an almost glass-like appearance.

As we stood back admiring our engineering marvel, Pete broke the silence by saying, "Okay, which one a you brave souls is gonna be first?"

For a moment, we all just looked at each other. Finally, Spike, spoke up, "Hell, I guess I can give it a shot."

Wally went up the hill with Spike to give him a push-start. The rest of waited off to the side of the ramp, where we could best see the action when Spike got airborne.

Looking up the hill, we watched as Spike climbed on the toboggan. Wally, straddling the middle of the toboggan, then clumsily pushed Spike about 15 feet, until the toboggan had enough momentum to go on its own. As the toboggan gained speed and headed downhill toward the foot of the ramp, it became more clear that Spike was not lined up properly.

The toboggan was now running at full speed and Pete was yelling frantically, "Lean left, Spike! Lean left, Goddamit!"

Apparently, Spike started his lean a little late, because when he hit the bottom of the ramp, he was too far right of center. The toboggan rose up quickly, but rolled to the right as it crossed over the front corner of the ramp. His eyes were huge as he became airborne and rose 10 feet above the ground, realizing the landing would not be what he had anticipated.

The toboggan came down nose-end first and made contact with its right-front corner about 25 feet in front of the ramp. The hard impact caused the toboggan to flip end-over-end, catapulting Spike further down the hill.

Miraculously, Spike was only dazed when we got to him. As Wally helped him to his feet, Spike stood on wobbly legs for a moment, then shook his head, and exclaimed proudly, "Damn, did ya see that freakin' flip I just made!"

"Yeah, but that ain't the way its 'sposed to be done," Pete fired back, revealing his agitation. "I just hope my toboggan's still in one piece," he added, as he turned and walked toward the inverted toboggan.

We all followed Pete to help inspect the condition of the toboggan. Surprisingly, the toboggan had survived the 'crash landing' about as well as Spike had. It was only scuffed a little on the curved surface along the left-front edge.

As the six of us trudged back up the hill, Spike asked nonchalantly, "Well, who's next?"

There was no response; just five blank stares.

"You buncha candy-asses!" Spike barked, as we reached the top of the hill. "Guess I'll just hafta do it again, myself."

"Wait just a damn minute, Spike," Pete said angrily. "You can bust your ass if you wanna, but you ain't gonna wreck my toboggan in the process. My dad'll kill me if it's messed up when I get home."

"Aw, c'mon, Pete," Spike pleaded. "I know what I did wrong. I'll get it right this time. What if I promise ta pay for any damages? Sound okay, huh?"

"Well, okay, I guess so," Pete said hesitantly. "But you be damn careful, and get it lined up this time or turn away from the ramp."

"No sweat," Spike responded. "You guys can go back down now and get ready to witness the perfect jump. Wally, you stay here and give me a shove."

We waited by the ramp, watching the scene at the top of the hill unfold. Wally seemed to give a better start this time, because Spike was flying at the halfway point. Fifty feet from the foot of the ramp he seemed to be lined up perfectly. Suddenly, he was on the ramp and gaining altitude.

As he broke the bonds of gravity and became airborne, a serene smile spread across his face. He knew this would be a good one!

We stood in awe as he rose nearly 15 feet in the air and then glided over 30 feet before landing softly on the snowy incline. His momentum carried him another 100 feet downhill, before coming to stop on the level part of the course. We cheered him loudly as he pulled the toboggan back up the hill. He was smiling triumphantly when he joined us at the ramp.

Smiling broadly, he asked "Well, whadda ya think, guys?"

"Man, that was some kinda ride," I said, reaching out to shake his hand.

"Yeah, an awesome display." Charlie added, almost pumping Spike's arm off.

"Well, I guess ya do know what you're doin' after all, Spike," Pete conceded, while shaking his hand.

"Man, you got some big balls," Wally said, slapping Spike on the back.

Bob, who didn't talk much, could only slap ol' Spike on the back, and smile admiringly at him.

With wide-eyed admiration, Wally asked, "Weren't ya scared even a little bit, Spike?"

"Hell no!" Spike proclaimed loudly, his chin jutting out arrogantly. "I'm the best there ever was."

Pete and I hoisted Spike to our shoulders and carried him the rest of the way to the top of the hill. The ear-to-ear grin that Spike displayed was proof enough that he was eating up the hero treatment.

At the top of the hill, we were greeted by Bud Chessman and Lowell Thornton, two more guys from the neighborhood.

"Hi, fellas. Mind if Lowell and I use your slidin' place?" Bud asked friendly-like.

"Well, okay, but ya gotta keep your sleds on another part of the hill," Pete replied. "We can't afford to have the toboggan course torn up after all the work we put into it."

"Sounds fair ta me," Bud said, grinning.

As we stood talking at the top of hill, three more guys arrived: Billy Joe Griffin, who lived about 10 blocks away, and two of his buddies, whom none of us knew. One of Billy Joe's friends was pulling a toboggan.

We welcomed the three and explained the course rules to them.

I think by this time we had all accepted the fact that we weren't going to be able to keep our sliding place a secret. More and more people arrived throughout the day. Before the day was over, there were five toboggans on our part of the hill and probably 35 to 40 sleds being used on another part of the hill.

By mid-afternoon, each of us from the original six members (Spike, Pete, Wally, Charlie, Bob, and I) had made a least one successful jump with the toboggan. Of course, there were more spills than successes.

Billy Joe and his two friends were also using the toboggan jump. Billy Joe, a daredevil in his own right, had mastered the jump quickly, and was actually becoming bored, because the challenge was beginning to wear off. He was a state-champion spring-board diver for the local YMCA swim team, so It must have been his flare for the acrobatic that prompted him to crave more daring feats.

Standing at top of the hill with the rest of us, Billy Joe boasted, "Hell, this is kid's stuff, goin' over the jump sittin' down. I think I'll try it standin' up."

Seemingly hurt by someone trying to steal his hero status, Spike's temper flared, "Billy Joe, you ain't got the guts to do the jump standin' up."

"Just stand up here with the other girls, where it's safe, and watch me," Billy Joe taunted.

Spike, his face red with anger, fumed, "Well, Smart Ass, if you can do it, so can I! Let's see your stuff."

Billy Joe was smiling confidently as he pushed his toboggan along scooter-style to get it started. Once the toboggan was moving on its own, he stood holding the pull rope for balance, looking very much like a Roman chariot driver.

"He'll never go through with it," Spike said smugly. "Nobody's that stupid."

We all ran down the hill after Billy Joe, to get a closer look at the spectacle in progress. All activity on the course abruptly ceased as the word got around. Everyone's eyes were focused on Billy Joe, who was now flashing down the hill, leaning right and left as necessary to bring the toboggan into perfect alignment.

He seemed to hit the foot of the ramp with exactness.

Billy Joe, however, couldn't resist the compulsion to show-boat as he shot off the end of the ramp. To make the moment even more glorious, he left go of the tow rope with his right hand in order to wave at the host of admiring fans below. It was at this moment, a good 15 feet above the ground, that a gust of wind moved the toboggan from under his feet. There was Billy Joe, beginning to tumble head-first to the frozen ground below, while the toboggan glided off to his right.

Billy Joe knew he was in big trouble as he grabbed his knees and pulled them into the tuck position. It was now obvious his diving instincts had taken over when he rolled completely over and opened up in a spread-eagle fashion to land flat on his back 30 feet down the course.

Everyone rushed to the scene. Billy Joe was beginning to stir when we got to him. The hard landing had knocked the air out of him and left him dazed.

As Pete helped Billy Joe to his feet, a tremendous cheer went up. Thunderous applause and cheering continued for a full two minutes.

Wally rushed up to Billy Joe and began pumping his arm. "I gotta say, that was the Goddamdest thing I ever did see, Billy Joe " he gushed.

As more hand-shaking and back-slapping ensued, I heard Spike mumble, "What the hell was so great about that, anyway? He couldn't even stay on the freakin' toboggan."

It was apparent we had us a new hero, and Spike didn't like it one bit.

At the top of the hill once more, Billy Joe goaded Spike by saying, "Okay, Big Man, it's your turn now."

Spike spit and sputtered, finally saying, "What I meant was I'd be willin' to try it if you'd a done it without screwin' up. Well, you screwed it up, so I don't hafta do it."

"I don't blame ya for bein' chicken-shit," Billy Joe taunted. "I don't think I'll be tryin' it anymore, myself."

That was the end of that. No one else dared to try the jump standing up.

Only one other noteworthy thing happened that afternoon. Bud Chessman, Lowell Thornton, and two other guys started down the course in a toboggan right ahead of Pete, Spike, Wally, and me in another toboggan. Lowell was the last man in the front toboggan.

About half way down the course, the first toboggan went over a bump, throwing Lowell out on the course directly in front of our toboggan. We made a desperate attempt to miss him as he rolled down hill. We were able to miss his upper body, but, unfortunately, our toboggan ran over his legs, spinning his body violently.

His toboggan and the three remaining team mates continued on down the course. We in the second toboggan immediately threw our feet out to the side and dug in our heels to brake our forward momentum. We were able to stop about 50 feet down the course from where Lowell lay moaning.

Lowell was sitting up and crying uncontrollably when we arrived on the scene. He was holding his right leg and refused to let anyone look at it. "Just help me get home!" he kept pleading.

"Aw, he ain't hurt bad." Spike said dispassionately. "Let 'im walk home."

"Then what's all that blood leakin' through his pant leg?" Pete shot back angrily.

"Oh, my God, you're right, Pete!" Spike exclaimed, seeing the blood pooling up in the snow. "Geez, I'm sorry, Lowell," Spike said remorsefully. "We'd better getcha home."

Pete and I locked our hands and wrists together, forming a seat for
Lowell. Spike and Wally gently pulled Lowell to his feet and hoisted
him onto the human seat we had fashioned.

Fortunately, Lowell lived only a half city-block from the Labs, so we
were there in less than 5 minutes. His mother, looking very worried,
met us at the back door. We carried Lowell into the kitchen and sat him
on a chair. He was moaning in pain by now, and white as a ghost.

After we'd explained what had happened to Lowell, Mrs. Thornton
quickly thanked us and told us good-bye and that we'd have to leave,
because she needed to call her doctor right away.

After the accident to Lowell, the four of us decided we'd had enough
sledding for the day.

Later that evening, Mrs. Thornton phoned my house to inform my
Mom that Lowell had broken his lower leg in two places, and that the
blood we'd seen was caused by an especially serious compound frac-
ture. After Mom told me the bad news, I immediately began calling the
other guys to inform them of the seriousness of the accident.

The following day, on our way to another toboggan outing, Pete,
Spike, Wally, and I stopped at Lowell's house to wish him well and to
sign his plaster cast. He had his color back and was looking markedly
better than he had the day before. He thanked us for coming to see him,
and informed us he'd be wearing the cast for at least six weeks and
would have to get around on crutches.

The word had spread all over town about the great sliding conditions
at the Harrington Labs hill. Somewhere between 150 and 200 kids
showed up the second day. The old hill was a beehive of activity until
late that evening.

I was surprised to find Reggie there when I returned home that
Friday evening. He explained that his boss had given most of the bakery crew the weekend off, because of the temporary business slowdown
that always follows Christmas.

"Whadda ya gonna do tonight, Reg?" I inquired.

"Oh, I think I'll just hang around the house and get to bed early." he
replied. "Ya know I've been workin' purty hard lately."

"For cryin' out loud!" I said, with a shocked expression. "That don't sound like much fun."

"Well, what are you gonna do that's so exciting?" he asked.

"I thought I'd get together with Spike and Wally and we'd take our sleds out and hook some car rides." I responded.

As I made that statement, an idea flashed through my mind: "Wait a minute, why don't you and me go out hookin' cars together?" I asked eagerly. "Heck, we ain't done nothin' together for a long time. Whadda ya say, Reg?"

"Well, I don't know." Reggie said, frowning. "I told ya before that I'm gettin too old for that kinda stuff. I'd feel kinda silly."

"C'mon, Reg, just once more, for ol' times' sake," I pleaded, trying to look as hurt as possible in hopes I could make him feel guilty.

Finally relenting, but none too happy, Reggie said, "Okay, okay, but only for an hour or so." Quickly changing his expression to one of confusion, he asked, "But what about Spike and Wally?"

"Heck, I can be with those guys anytime. But tonight it's just you and me, Big Brother." I replied, draping my arm over his shoulder.

It wasn't long before we were outside in the brisk night air, pulling our sleds in the direction of the downtown area.

The object of "Hooking" is to be able to grab the rear bumper of a car while it's stopped and then let the car pull you along on your sled.

This procedure is accomplished by waiting on the sidewalk at an intersection where cars are required to stop, either by a traffic light or stop sign. Preferably, the intersection is not a busy one, because too many cars can make the act even more risky than it's intended to be.

When the target car has stopped, the "Hooker" sneaks around to the rear of the vehicle and lays on down on his sled, with one hand on the sled's steering arm and the other firmly grasping the car's bumper. After that, it's just a matter of waiting for the car to take off, and then enjoying the ride until another convenient stop is made.

After about a half an hour, Reggie and I had successfully hooked enough cars to transport us to the west side of town and back, probably four miles round-trip.

We were at the intersection of Lipton and Division Streets, about five blocks from home, when we decided to take one more ride in a westerly direction. We waited in the shadows on east side of the intersection for not more than five minutes before a commercial panel truck pulled to a stop.

As Reggie and I sneaked around to the rear of the truck, I noticed the printing on its side: "Spath's Florist Shoppe." Before the light turned green, I stood up for a moment and peeked inside through one of the small rear windows. I immediately recognized the driver to be Bob Spath, the 18-year-old son of the flower shop owner.

As I lay back down on my sled, I shared my discovery with Reggie. Reggie just whispered, "So what, he's just probably returnin' to the shop from makin' a flower delivery. Hell, we can ride this one all the way to the west side of town, where the flower shop is."

Just then the light turned green, and the panel truck shot away from the intersection as if it were in a drag race. The tires squealed each time a new gear grabbed hold, as the driver shifted rapidly to attain maximum acceleration.

"What the hell!" I exclaimed, as I looked over to Reggie, whose eyes seemed to popping from his head.

We were already speeding down the narrow street at what seemed to be at least 45 mph, when Reggie looked at me and yelled, "I think the son-of-a-bitch knows we're back here. He's just tryin' to scare us."

"Well, he's sure doin' a helluva job," I thought to myself.

Even though the ride was terrifying at this point, we couldn't leave go of the bumper. There were too many cars traveling in the opposite direction and parked cars lined the right side of the street.

We were going so fast at one point that we were literally lifted off the ground as the truck careened around a sharp curve.

The worst was yet to come. After about five blocks, the street surface suddenly turned from ice and snow to just bare bricks. As showers of sparks flew off our sled runners, the tug on our arms became almost unbearable. We both gritting our teeth in an effort to hold on.

After one-half block of dry pavement, we were suddenly back on an icy surface. It was then that Reggie looked at me, almost apologetically, and yelled, "I gotta let go. Wish me luck."

At that instant he released his grip and was abruptly propelled in an arc to the right, barely missing a parked car as he shot up and over the curb.

Still hanging on to the bumper and straining to peer back over my shoulder, I caught a glimpse of Reggie as he flew up over a small hill and crashed into a flower bed that lined the front porch of a brick house. The last I saw of him he seemed to be laying motionless on his back, entangled in a mass of garden stakes.

I was almost grief-stricken as I pondered how badly Reggie may be hurt. I was also terrified thinking about my own predicament.

My salvation came to me in a flash as I flew down Lipton Street: *"Hey, I might still be able to survive this ordeal,"* I thought. *"There's a stop sign coming up at Main Street, only a block and a half ahead."*

When the flower truck came to a screeching stop at Main Street, I quickly jumped to my feet and, grabbing my sled with one hand, started running as fast as I could in the other direction.

As I made my "getaway," I could hear the 18-year-old truck driver laughing raucously. With his head stuck out the window, and looking back in my direction, he yelled, "How did ya like that ride, Sonny?"

I looked back as the truck pulled through the intersection, just in time to see my right glove, which was frozen to the bumper and still maintaining my original death-grip.

As I approached the area where I'd seen Reggie crash, I fully expected to see him still lying in the flower bed. I was overjoyed to see him standing there on the street corner waiting for me — even though he was battered and bruised somewhat, and his sled was in two pieces.

As we walked home, Reggie, who was limping noticeably, didn't seem too angry about the mess I'd gotten him into and even chuckled as he said, "Dammit, I told ya I was gettin' too old for this kid stuff."

Reggie was right, I thought to myself. I, too, needed to take on a more serious nature. Heck, in only a week I would turn 14, much too old for those childish antics.

This was truly the last time that Reggie and I would do kid stuff together. It can also be stated with certainty that the other guys and I would never again experience a year like 1945.

Reflecting on this period more than a half-century later, it now seems as if this band of young men subconsciously knew they were reaching the secret age of accountability and were rushing to cram in as much adventure as possible, and, now that this passion had been satiated, could get on with the business of growing up.

This is not to say that the guys and I had lost our zest for life. Oh no! There were many more fun times throughout our high school years; but admittedly, none that could hold a candle to "Growin' Up in '45."

The End

ABOUT THE AUTHOR

The author, Max Geyer, was born and raised in a small town in Indiana. He completed his first 12 years of education in the Catholic school system.

During the Korean War, he honorably served a four-year enlistment in the U.S. Navy.

After completion of his military duty, he began work as an electronics technician. He later married, and he and his wife, Lucy, raised three children.

Max ultimately worked a total of 32 years in the technical publications field, before retiring in 1992. In retirement, he was able to author his first book — *Growin' Up in '45*.

Printed in the United States
30699LVS00003B/223-252

9 780595 000791